DRAMA DEMON

UNDERTOWN PARANORMAL MYSTERIES
BOOK 2

TABATHA GRAY

ISBN: 978-1-960062-01-7

Author site: www.tabathagray.com

Editing by Whitney Morsillo, Anne Cousins, and Victory Editing

Cover Design by Mariah Sinclair www.mariahsinclair.com

This book was written and is set in the traditional land of the first people of Seattle, the Duwamish People past and present. We honor with gratitude the land itself and the Duwamish Tribe.

AUTHOR'S NOTE

Did you know you can get exclusive messages from Undertown sent right to your email? It's like having a friend giving you the neighborhood gossip as you read.

If you picked up this book through my website, tabathagray.com, the bonuses will start arriving in your inbox just a day or so after your purchase.

And if you bought the book elsewhere, no worries at all! You can still get the read-along experience by visiting tabathagray.com/utbonus. Enjoy!

CHAPTER 1
DREAM HOUSE

"Oh my god. How am I ever going to get through all my aunt's files?" said Emma, looking up from the pile of old manila folders that lay around her on the floor. One folder was open, spilling out a jumble of notes, printouts, photos. She looked up at the ceiling where Viv was on a ladder, addressing a Frankenstein's monster of drywall patches. "And Thanksgiving's in a week! How are we ever going to finish this?"

"So, uh, about that," Viv said as she plopped a mound of drywall mud onto the ceiling. If you ignored the faint mildew smell, you almost couldn't tell the pipes had burst or that the room had been a lake just a few weeks ago. "This might go a little faster if—"

Beep. Beep. Beep.

Emma looked up, grinning. "Hold that thought." She stood and rushed out of the room, down the hall, and into the kitchen.

Her kitchen.

If the dining room was a nightmare, the kitchen was a dream: white cabinets, tile floor, and a butcher-block countertop polished to a golden sheen. A stainless-steel fridge sat against one wall along with a matching oven and dishwasher. Near the door was a small breakfast table with four padded seats. It had cost a pretty penny, but it was worth it.

She pressed a button on the microwave, and the beeping stopped. She opened the oven door.

"I think they're ready!" she called back, her cheeks rosy from the oven's heat. She reached in and pulled out a tray of chocolate chip cookies.

She gingerly placed the hot cookie sheet on the stove and produced a little box of Maldon salt, dropping a few of the fluffy crystals on each cookie.

"Those smell amazing," Viv said as she walked in. The smell of buttery, brown-sugar-infused cookie wafted through the air.

They would be too hot to eat, but *what the heck*? Emma handed one to Viv and took one for herself. As she bit into it, her eyes shut. It was everything she'd hoped for: chewy, rich —sweet and salty all at once. It tasted like pure comfort.

She had finally broken her baking curse. Maybe Thanksgiving wouldn't be a disaster after all.

Her shoulders relaxed, and a smile stretched across her face. When she opened her eyes, Viv was grinning at her from around a bite of cookie. "So, like I was saying, I told you that I'd be happy to show you how to do your drywall project. But it seems like I've been doing it all myself."

Emma's face fell. "You're right. I'm sorry. I just have so much to do! I'm so stressed out about hosting Thanksgiving, and the house is falling apart."

"You really want your mom to see you're doing okay out here, huh?"

"Yes! And how was I to know that as soon as I sent the invite, the plumbing in my dining room would break open like the Hoover Dam? And Dash is on my case about his stuff…"

"Is he that bad?"

"He's just… persistent. Ever since I helped Alice Beyer's spirit pass through the veil, he thinks that I can do the same for him. I don't know what to do. I thought maybe if I read all my aunt's old case files…"

"Really, there weren't any? I would have thought a psychic would be helping spirits pass through the veil left and right."

"Maybe she did, but there's nothing in the files so far. Just lots of kids falling down wells. Lots of satanists—"

"Um, what?"

"It was the eighties. Satanic panic. I don't think they were real. Same with most of the demonic possessions after *The Exorcist* came out."

"Oh yeah, I remember that. My aunt Flo got convinced she was possessed by a demon that spoke Italian."

"Italian?"

"Not real Italian. She just *started a-talking like-a Super Mario*. Waved her hands a lot."

Emma laughed and settled into a relaxed smile—then a shadow passed across her face. It deepened into a frown.

"With Alice, the answer just fell in my lap. Once she learned about her past and was able to accept that it really happened to her and wasn't her fault, she was able to move on."

"So why not help Dash find out about his past?"

"It's different. I had Alice's diary. I don't have anything like that for Dash. And when he gets close to remembering, he kind of blanks out."

"I'll tell you what," Viv said around another bite of cookie. "Since you have so much going on right now, I'll keep helping you with your drywall."

"Really? Oh, that's amazing. Thank you so much!"

"But, uh, Emma—I think you might need a little more practice on these cookies."

"Really? I thought they were—"

"I think you should practice making them every day. Around the time I come over to do drywall."

"Meow."

Both turned to see the massive brindle cat peeking around the edge of the kitchen door. He had a notched ear, a snaggle-tooth, and a scar running across one eye.

"Afternoon, Captain," Viv said.

The cat stepped into the room and meandered over to them to rub up against Emma's leg. She bent down and petted him. He purred loudly, his tail whipping back and forth across her arm.

"I can't believe the captain lets you pet him like that," Viv said, using a spatula to peel another cookie off the sheet.

"We have a relationship of mutual admiration—and I give him all the cream he wants." Emma walked to the fridge. She took out a ceramic jug of cream and poured some into a dish.

Stepping out of the kitchen, she walked to the door under the stairs. It was small, made of polished oak, and very sturdy. Cut into the bottom was a plastic cat flap.

Opening the door, she saw the captain's Victorian study. It was exactly how it had been in Aunt Cora's house. Miniature oil paintings of sailing ships hung on miniature papered walls. Miniature bookcases held fine, leather-bound miniature books. On a mahogany side table was a decanter of brandy and two brandy snifters.

An oxblood armchair sat slightly askew in front of a large miniature desk with a miniature typewriter and a messy stack of pages. On the floor next to the desk was an empty saucer.

She took the empty dish and replaced it with the full one. The captain began to lap up the cream.

"Meow." The captain looked up reproachfully.

"I know. I know," Emma replied. "You need your edits. I'll get them to you. I've just been so busy. I thought that once I quit my job, I'd have a few less people pulling at me, but I'm stretched thinner than ever."

Emma closed the door to give the captain some privacy. Ever since he and his compatriots of the night watch had driven all the rats out of Undertown, he had adopted the life of a gentleman of leisure and was focusing on his writing.

A familiar voice called out. "Hello? Is anyone home?"

Oh God, were they late? Emma froze. She looked at Viv, who was standing in the doorway to the kitchen, guiltily chewing her third cookie.

"What time is it?"

"Microwave says it's one—"

"That clock's wrong. I forgot to set it!"

"We installed that thing a month ago. Who doesn't set their clock?"

"I don't apparently." Emma raced to her purse, which was hanging off a dining table chair. She rummaged around and pulled out her phone. The time on the screen read 2:35 p.m. Her heart sank.

CHAPTER 2
LATE

She'd gotten so caught up in renovations, chatting with Viv, reading her aunt's old files, and baking cookies that she'd—

"Hello? Emma? Oh, there you are," the man said, grinning. He was tall with dark, slicked-back hair and shy eyes that seemed large against his thin face. His tweed suit was perfectly pressed, his bow tie expertly knotted, and his hair parted so sharply it could cut glass. From his jacket pocket hung a pocket-watch chain.

"Hi, Dash! Sorry, I've been running like a chicken with its head cut off."

"Oh, is Dash here?" Viv said, looking up and waving. "Hi, Dash!"

"You're not waving at Dash, Viv. He's, um, over here." It was still a little weird being able to see *dead people*. It was even weirder that folks believed her. Her family had a reputation though. "I completely lost track of time. Has it started?"

"No, actually. The cast seems to be… well, locked out."

"Someone locked them out?"

"Strange things have been happening. Items going missing. For example, Riley's laptop. I wanted to see if they'd lost it here."

"Their laptop? I don't think—"

"Hey, Em, isn't that it under those magazines?"

"What do you know? It is," Emma said, pulling the computer from under a bunch of old issues of *Scientific American*.

"Excellent. Would you mind, er, carrying it there?" Dash held up his hands and shrugged. Spirits like him tended to pass through anything they touched.

"No problem," Emma said, stuffing the laptop into her bag. She turned to Viv. "Ready?"

They stopped in the hallway in front of the captain's study.

"You coming, Captain?" Emma called, but the only reply was the sound of the captain's manual typewriter. "Suit yourself, but it'd do you good to get out a little more."

Emma and Viv stopped at the front door, put on their raincoats, then headed out into Undertown.

Undertown was a neighborhood in Seattle, but you wouldn't find it on any ordinary map. Due to a heady mix of history, magic, and legal obstinacy, the neighborhood had remained independent for the past century as Seattle grew around it and encased it like a pearl.

Emma's house sat near the very heart of that pearl. It was an area that, due to a misfired spell decades ago, had been cursed and barren. Over time, it was becoming lush and green again, aided by the mild temperatures and the soothing rain.

Beyond this core was New Main Street: a circular avenue filled with cozy shops, delicious restaurants, and good friends. Beyond that were the hills—large rises filled with trees, homes, and blackberry briars.

Emma breathed deeply. The air was soothing, cool, and

damp. The smell of wet earth and greenery hung in the air, and a thin veil of moisture glistened on leaves and grass. Ahead, a robin dipped its beak into the ground, looking for worms.

"I can't believe they're trying to restore it," Viv said.

"Restore what? Sorry, I was just thinking about how different this place looks now."

"The theater," Viv said, nodding her head toward the old building to their right. "It just seems like such a big project, ya know?"

"Riley said it was well-preserved. They only needed to turn on the utilities. I just hope its pipes don't burst."

"Ha! It's already hard enough to find a plumber."

Emma glanced toward the theater. The building was old, built over a hundred years ago. The facade was covered in elaborate carvings of statues of lions and eagles rising to claw at the sky. The windows were tall and arched, framed in stone that had been carved to look like vines and flowers.

"It's... kind of creepy." Emma said.

"I remember when it opened," said Dash.

"Really? Did it look creepy then?"

"No, it was marvelous. If they manage to restore it to its original opulence, it will be a sight to behold."

"What show did you see there?" Emma asked.

"I... You know, I don't recall. It was—" Dash flickered out of existence for a moment. "Did I just..."

"You disappeared again. Only for a second."

"It's quite frustrating."

"Just relax if you can. We're here to enjoy ourselves," Emma said, looking back toward the theater.

She let her eyes follow the vines up to the top of the facade, where at the very top was a pair of stone gargoyles looking down onto the street below. One gargoyle was hunched forward, its wings curved around its body like a protective cloak. Its head was tilted down, and its eyes burned with an inner fire. Its mouth was a twisted snarl, filled with sharp teeth that looked like they could rip through stone.

It winked at her.

CHAPTER 3
THEY'LL PAY

"This stress is getting to me. I'm seeing things," muttered Emma.

"Isn't that, like, your jam?" Viv asked. "You see things other people can't? You have whole conversations with them—"

"No, this was different. It wasn't a spirit. It was just—Never mind. Did Riley ever find a place to rent in the neighborhood?" Emma asked. "They've really jumped into being part of the community with the theater and everything."

"No," Viv shook her head. "They haven't been able to find any place they can afford."

"But… I mean, look at all these empty houses!"

The sidewalk led them to a turn that led out of the core. When this place had been cursed, you could get lost here for days.

"After forty years, it's not so easy to track down the owners. Heck, when I was a kid, the next-door neighbor died, but he didn't leave a will, and nobody could figure out who owned the house."

"What happened to it?"

"Nothing for a long time. Then the roof fell in. Rotted

through, I guess. It's… weird to me that all these buildings have held up."

"They say magic has unpredictable side effects."

The alley was narrow and dark. The walls were rough and unadorned brick, mortar crumbling away to reveal the rough stone underneath.

"I told you; I'm not interested in your money!" a man's voice echoed around the corner.

There was silence. Then a calmer, quieter voice replied.

"You need to end it now—or I will. I promise you; the whole organization will pay for what they've done to my family."

Viv turned to Emma. "Should we… find another way to the community center?"

"We're already late. We don't have time to take the long way."

Dash disappeared around the corner, then came back a moment later.

"It's Brutus and Caesar—I mean Clarence and Harold."

"Do I know them?"

"Clarence? The chairman of the Undertown Neighborhood Association?"

"Oh, that Clarence."

"No time! We have to go!"

"Wasn't Clarence—" Viv began, but Emma had already plunged ahead.

They rounded the corner and found the tall man, Harold, in the process of departing. Clarence was still there, breathing heavily and looking at the ground. His hands were balled into fists at his sides. He was wearing—of all things—a toga.

He heard them, looked up, and sighed. "Oh, it's you, Ms. Day." His face was red, his lips pressed tight. His hands shook as he tried to smooth his hair down. "Are you going to the show?" He forced a smile. "I should be getting back."

"We're going, yeah."

"Well, enjoy the show. It's time people learn what stuff Clarence is made of." He quickly walked away as they watched him go.

"Well… that was intense," Viv said.

"Before I moved here, I never would have guessed there would be so much drama packed into such a small neighborhood."

"Mrow!"

Emma turned around. "So you decided to join us, did you? I think we just might make it in time if we're fast enough."

"Meow." The cat purred and rubbed against Emma's leg.

A few moments later, they joined the crowd waiting at the venue. The normally plain, dilapidated storefront of the Undertown Community Center had been transformed for the afternoon into the facade of the Undertown Community Theater.

The sidewalk was crowded with theatergoers who milled around, ignoring the drizzle like true Seattleites. Some chatted with friends, others waited impatiently for the doors to open. The air was thick with the smell of popcorn and perfume.

"Do you think they found the key?"

"Not sure why people would be hanging out here if they did."

There was a murmur in the crowd. The front doors opened, but they quickly closed again. The crowd parted, and a small intense person with a trendy mullet pushed through, looking left and right. Riley.

Riley's gaze fixed on Emma, Viv, and the captain. "Oh thank God, you're here. Did you bring my computer? Is Dash back? Has anyone seen my Brutus?"

"You mean Clarence? We saw him on the way here. Didn't he come this way?"

"If I didn't know better, I'd say this play was cursed. I'm

missing my Caesar and my Brutus. I left my computer at your house. My walkie-talkie is missing. The scripts and blocking instructions are missing."

"Maybe it *is* cursed," Viv offered.

"There are twenty-eight distinct orders in the taxonomy of curses. I did my doctoral dissertation on them. This situation doesn't fall under any of them—although…"

Just then, Clarence arrived. "Sorry, sorry!" the man called out, jogging toward them. "I had a little problem to take care of.

"Chairman!" a woman in the crowd called out, coming toward them. Her hair was styled in soft waves and fell to her shoulders. Her nails were polished a deep red, and she wore a cashmere sweater set against a backdrop of pearls. She approached him, adjusted his toga, then gave him a quick kiss. "Break a leg, sugar."

Clarence whispered something to her, and then he headed toward the gate that led to the community center's rear entrance.

"She's putting out some serious Stepford vibes," Viv said to Emma, low enough not to be overheard.

"He has a wife? I assumed that after the Neighborhood Association meetings, he went home to hibernate in some kind of beige vat."

Emma glanced over at the woman. The woman looked back at them, slightly flushed, and stepped back, adjusting the purse on her arm. Emma felt a pang of jealousy and a pang of something else too—something like longing for these people's boring, normal life.

The woman waited for a moment, then turned and walked away.

CHAPTER 4
POP GOES THE WEASEL

"All right, everybody! No pushing. There's room for everyone. No tickets required, but as you come in, you'll notice a merch counter and donation area to your right. Everything we make here will go toward restoring the old theater. Next time we stage Shakespeare, it will be in a real theater!"

Dash turned to Emma. "I need to go prepare the atmospherics."

"Break a leg," she said and turned to Viv. "Dash is taking off."

"Bye, Dash." Viv waved even though he had already gone. "It's really cool that he's found a way to be involved despite his... not having a body."

"Turns out the dead are great at atmospherics."

A cheer went up as the crowd began pushing forward. Viv led the way. The doors parted, and they stepped into the foyer of the community center turned community theater.

A papier-mâché chandelier hung from the ceiling, and a red carpet lined the floor. The walls were lined with portraits of past presidents of the Neighborhood Association.

Beside the merch table, a woman in a red dress stood

holding a clipboard. Her hair was pinned up in a complicated chignon, lipstick perfectly applied. Next to her was a man with a receding hairline, dressed in an ill-fitting suit. He leaned against the wall near an old-fashioned pay phone, looking like he wanted to be anywhere else on earth.

The woman waved them over. "Hey, guys."

"Um… Astrid? I didn't recognize you for a second. You look great!" Emma exclaimed.

"I figured why not look nice for the opening night—er, matinee? Anyway, here are your programs. You can pick any seats you like. Enjoy the show!"

"Thanks!"

The seats were surprisingly full for the first day of a small-town performance. A few heads turned as they entered and found chairs in the back row.

Astrid took the stage and introduced the director, Riley, who walked out to a round of applause.

"Today, we'll be performing *Julius Caesar* for you," Riley said to the crowd. "Our group has worked really hard on it. I hope you like it."

Then the room went dark.

"It's really so odd, having two partners at the firm engaged in such a spectacle," an imperious woman's voice hissed in the row behind where Emma and her friends sat.

"I suppose when you rise enough in the world, you can stop caring a bit about what people think."

"Can you? I should hardly imagine that the institutions engaging the most prestigious accounting firm in the Pacific Northwest should be happy to hear that the partners were gallivanting around on stage like a pair of little boys."

"Oh, calm down, Miriam. It's not as if they're staging *Oscar Wilde*. This is Shakespeare. It is respectable. And Harold Loftus playing Caesar no less. One could hardly imagine a more august role—"

The stage lights rose. The audience sat in darkness, and

the crowd stilled. The curtain opened to reveal a minimalist set made of red and black panels.

A spotlight shone down on a small group of men standing on stage. One man stood in a red cape and toga among the group of other rougher-looking characters. The audience was silent, the only sounds the voice of the man on stage and the soft rustling of programs being turned.

"Hence! Home, you idle creatures, get you home! Is this a holiday? What, know you not, being mechanical, you ought not walk upon a laboring day without the sign of your profession? Speak, what trade art thou?"

Even though the actor was no professional, Emma felt herself being pulled into the world he was creating. She couldn't help it. That's what stories did to her. She leaned forward in her seat.

"Psst. Emma." It was Dash. "There's a problem. Come with me."

Emma whispered an excuse and followed Dash out into the hallway. She blinked in the sudden brightness.

An older woman in a gray pantsuit lay sprawled upon the ground. Her purse sat open next to her. Emma stared at her for a moment before she realized it was Darla, one of the board members on the Neighborhood Association. She wasn't moving.

Emma's mouth dropped open. "Is she—?"

"I'm not dead! I twisted my ankle. Get over here and help me up!"

Emma helped her sit, leaning against the wall. "What happened?"

"What happened? I'm old is what happened. These heels are made for younger women."

"Do you need to go to the hospital?"

"I need to get to my seat. But first, be a doll and fetch me some ibuprofen from the first aid kit? It should be in one of those drawers." She gestured toward an old desk.

"Of course." Emma walked over to the heavy wooden desk. It was dark wood, the surface scarred and battered from years of use. The chair behind it was old, its wood cracked and discolored. A brass lamp sat on one side, a messy stack of papers on the other. Emma searched the drawers one by one and eventually found a white metal box with a green cross emblazoned on the side. She set it on top of the desk and flipped the metal clasps up. "I found it. Just a sec and—"

The opening lid caused a sparkling cloud to burst from the box. The first aid kit was filled with glitter!

She felt a prickle in her nose. Oh no! She sneezed. A cloud of sparkling glitter flew into Emma's face, onto her clothes, into her hair.

"Where's the ibuprofen?"

"I… don't think there's any in there," Emma said.

"Oh my, you look like hell. Just don't get any of that on me when you take me to my seat."

Emma gave the woman her hand and steadied her as she pulled up to her knees. She let out a sharp hiss, and Emma found herself supporting most of her weight. Fortunately, she was as light as a bird with hollow bones.

They managed to awkwardly push open the auditorium door. Emma led her to a vacant seat in the back and went to rejoin her friends.

CHAPTER 5
ET TU BRUTE?

"What happened to you?" Viv sputtered.

"Shhhh!" someone behind them hissed.

Emma ignored Viv and looked toward the stage. It was filled with eerie, glowing fog. *Good work, Dash.*

Spirits couldn't touch or move anything or really do much at all. But they were amazing with atmospherics. Nothing like a little light haunting to set a vibe.

The audience sat lit only by the mist. A drumbeat sounded, and a spotlight illuminated a lone figure in a purple toga. The spotlight cast the man's features in deep relief. His high forehead and aquiline nose could have been carved from marble.

Emma leaned forward, drawn into the moment. A man in a toga approached the center figure.

"Most high, most mighty, and most puissant Caesar, Metellus Cimber throws before thy seat an humble heart—"

The man in purple lazily turned away from him. "I must prevent thee, Cimber. These couchings and these lowly courtesies might fire the blood of ordinary men…"

Another figure approached from the other side, pleading, "Is there no voice more worthy than my own to sound more sweetly in great Caesar's ear for the repealing of my banished brother?"

Then a third man entered the scene. It was Clarence, but he was acting nothing like the usual Clarence. No longer the mousy bureaucrat with the droning voice. He projected poise and confidence. "I kiss thy hand, but not in flattery, Caesar, desiring thee that Publius Cimber may have an immediate freedom of repeal."

"I could be well moved, if I were as you. If I could pray to move, prayers would move me. But I am constant as the northern star, of whose true fixed and resting quality there is no fellow in the firmament. The skies are painted with unnumbered sparks; they are all fire, and every one doth shine."

Emma frowned in confusion, turning to Viv. "What's going on?"

"Okay. The guy in the middle is Caesar. He's thrown someone in jail. The other guys want him released."

She squinted. It was Harold, standing in the middle. "That's not going to end well."

"Don't you know this story?" Viv sounded incredulous. "Oh, here it comes."

The actors were kneeling around Caesar now. Then one stood, pulling out a dagger.

"Speak, hands, for me!" His dagger hit, and the other senators attacked Caesar, raining down knife strokes as the drumbeat shook the floor.

Then Clarence, who had been standing aloof, approached Caesar, dagger drawn.

Caesar pointed at him with a shaking hand. "Et tu, Brute? Then fall, Caesar."

Clarence raised it high, then plunged it down into Harold's chest.

The drumbeat stopped. The scene went black.

"Harold? Harold!" Clarence's voice rang out. "Oh God. Turn on the lights! Somebody call an ambulance!"

The lights came on. Clarence stood over the body; his hands were covered in blood, and he still held the knife in his right hand. The audience sat in stunned silence.

"Is… this part of the play?" Viv whispered.

Clarence's eyes widened, and the knife clattered to the floor, breaking the stillness.

The crowd erupted into chaos as people pushed for the door. Riley rushed onto the stage, assessing the scene. Astrid handed them a microphone. "Do we have a doctor in the house?"

There apparently was, because a man from the audience jumped up to the stage and began ministering to the victim.

Then the room began to shake. A cold wind blew past Emma's cheek. The air smelled like ozone. It felt electric. Like just before a lightning strike.

"Hey, Em…" Viv was talking, but her voice was drowned out by the sound of rushing wind and water. Everything around her was statically charged, ready to blow and to rip apart reality into pieces swirling around her.

She knew this feeling.

"Um, Harold?" she asked.

The rushing sound grew louder. It was like she was in the middle of her own personal tornado that only affected her. She closed her eyes. The floor shook, and the lights flickered. The roof caved in. The walls blew out. Darkness and storm surrounded her, cold and wet. Her hair whipped around her face, slapping her cheeks.

She opened her eyes. The room was there, full of panicked people but otherwise unchanged.

She closed her eyes again. The shadowy figure who stood over the body of the dead man turned and looked at her. As he lunged at her, a flash of lightning split the sky and briefly illuminated his face before he disintegrated into shards of shattered ice that melted on her hot face.

A single word rang in her ears and filled the world: *Traitor!*

She opened her eyes. The stage was empty of people… unless you counted Caesar there, lying under the sheet.

Viv was waving a hand in front of Emma's face. The rushing sound grew quieter.

"…earth to Emma."

She shook her head and blinked. The room came into focus. Her eyes darted around, taking everything in. "Sorry, I just… I think I saw Harold's spirit leave his body."

"I guess that wasn't… fun."

"No. Not fun. What's that sound? Is someone crying?" Emma asked, turning. It was Gladys, stuck in her chair while everyone fled, unable to walk because of her bad ankle. "I'm going to help Gladys."

"Sounds good. I'm going to see if Riley needs an extra pair of hands."

As Emma stood, she swooned, still a little dizzy from her… encounter. After a few seconds, she was able to make her way back to Gladys, who was… laughing?

"He finally did it!" the woman said, grinning ear to ear. "I didn't think he had it in him, but he did it!" She grabbed Emma's arm and began hauling herself up. "Now we can get out of here. We're burning daylight. You're helping me home, aren't you? Wouldn't want to let a little old lady get hurt."

———

It had begun to drizzle. At the door, Emma put on her raincoat and helped Gladys with hers. The old woman took her time, fumbling with the buttons. Then they were off.

"My apartment is only a few blocks from here. I hope it's

no trouble," Gladys said, going back into her little-old-lady routine.

"It's not. I just have to ask. You seemed almost happy about what happened back at the theater."

"What? Oh, well, I was," Gladys said with a sideways smile. "Murder is a sin of course, but some people deserve it. That man had it coming."

"What did he do to you?"

"To me? Ha! Nothing. But to Clarence? Everything. What do you know about Caesar, dear?"

"Caesar?"

"I mean Harold of course. Senior partner to Clarence's junior at the accounting firm. The man strung Clarence along for years. Dangling promotion in front of him and jerking it away at the last moment. Making him go to more and more humiliating lengths to keep his place at the firm."

"There are people who do that?"

"Oh, Emma, you're lucky if you haven't met them. Even this play. Harold knew that Clarence was auditioning for the part of Caesar, so he swooped in and took it from him. He probably bribed the director."

Emma frowned. It was difficult to imagine someone bribing Riley for a part in a play. "So... what do you think will happen now?"

"It seems pretty cut-and-dried. We all saw Clarence do it. He's probably getting arrested now."

Emma frowned, thinking of her own too-recent run-ins with Undertown's confusing system of government. "I thought Undertown didn't have a police force."

"You're right of course. What I meant is that Marcus will drive him over to the county jail. Of course it's ridiculous we don't have a real police force. With any luck, that will change. You have no idea, Emma, the lengths people have gone to in blocking progress for this community."

The old woman stopped in front of a low, two-story apartment building. The building was old, the white paint peeling off in large strips to reveal the red brick beneath. A set of iron stairs led up to the front door, and a narrow window looked out onto the street from above it. There was a buzzer was next to a peeling sign that read APARTMENTS FOR RENT.

"This is my stop," Gladys said. "You really have been a dear."

"Do you have anyone at home to help you?"

"I suppose my husband might be some help if I can drag him out if his garage. I tell you, a man hits retirement age, and he thinks he's eighteen again."

"So that's a yes?"

"Don't you worry about me. You've been too kind as it is."

CHAPTER 6
CREMA

The community center was locked when Emma returned. She guessed they were at Deadtown, Viv's coffee shop, so Emma headed there.

Now that Gladys was no longer demanding her help, the enormity of what she had seen landed on her like a ton of bricks.

Clarence, that banal little man who presided over the Neighborhood Association meetings like a bad wedding emcee, had murdered his boss in cold blood—in front of everyone!

She turned, leaving the broad main street lined with shops and trees and turning in to an alley. Walls of weathered red brick rose around her, all peeling paint and crumbling mortar. If you looked up, you could make out traces of an old bait-and-tackle advertisement that had been painted on the brick decades ago but which had mostly peeled off.

Even in the November gloom, she wasn't as scared as the first time she came here. Then, even in the long summer twilight, the shadows held a certain impenetrable malevolence. You were likely to run into those weird rats. They'd kept their distance, but you always had the impression they were watching you.

The smell of coffee hit her as she turned the corner. A small concrete staircase led down to a heavy steel door painted green. A sign above the door read UNDERTOWN COFFEE ROASTERS. Above it was an old-fashioned gaslight, currently off.

Emma descended the stairs, pushed open the heavy door, and stepped inside. She paused to let her eyes adjust to the warm, dim light. A row of small round tables with thick wood chairs sat on one side of the room, a large counter on the other. The room was full of people sitting at tables, drinking coffee, and talking.

Her eyes adjusted to the light, and she spotted her friends all sitting around a green velvet sofa. She paused for a moment, taking off her raincoat, letting the room's warmth seep into her skin and soak into her bones.

She waved to her friends and approached the counter, where a purple-haired barista was sliding a huge mug of coffee to another customer. "Hey, Laney," Emma greeted the barista.

"Howdy, Emma. You're... shiny."

Emma looked down at her shirt and pants. They were still covered in glitter. She could see a little trail of it leading back to the door. "The play was... something."

"Yeah, from what I hear, I'm glad I didn't go. Everyone is over there processing. It sounds awful."

"To be honest, we didn't see much. It just seemed like part of the play."

"Well, there's nothing to bring you back to yourself like a cup of fine coffee. What can I get you?"

"One of those big lattes. The ones that come in a cup the size of a bowl."

"Central Perk size. Got you."

She grabbed the portafilter and twisted it off the gleaming chrome espresso machine. She placed it under the grinder and pressed a button, which filled it with the perfect amount of ground coffee beans—

"That's weird," the barista said.

"What?"

"The grounds don't look right." She raised the portafilter up and gingerly sniffed it. "They don't smell right either. Just a sec—"

She grabbed a second portafilter and filled it with grounds from a different grinder, examining it closely. "Oh no, I must have gotten the caffeinated and decaffeinated coffee beans mixed up when I filled the grinders this morning." She sighed. "No wonder everybody looks so groggy. It's okay. We'll give you the good stuff."

Then she pressed the caffeinated grounds down with a smooth steel tamper and put the whole thing back onto the machine. White crema and dark, rich espresso began to pour down a curved metal spout and into a ceramic vessel below. While it brewed, Laney steamed the milk. The thick, creamy milk went into an enormous ceramic cup, followed by the espresso.

"No latte art today, sorry. It's too hard with these big cups," she said, sliding the cup to Emma.

"No problem. It tastes the same. Put it on my tab?" Emma picked up the latte and sipped. The thick, rich liquid filled her mouth with its dark flavor. She could feel the warmth spreading out through her body, chasing away the chill that had been there ever since she helped Gladys home.

Emma let out a sigh, enjoying a moment of quiet, then walked over to the sofa where her friends were gathered around an electric fireplace.

"...I'm telling you, it's not your fault," Viv said.

"It feels like my fault. I was the director. It was my job to make sure all my actors were safe."

"From holes in the stage. It's not your job to keep them

from killing each other— Oh hey, Em," Viv said, noticing Emma's presence. "What happened to you?"

The whole group turned to look at her. Viv, Riley, Dash, Astrid, and a few other people Emma knew only vaguely were there. Only the captain, who was perched on the coffee table, licking a bowl of cream, didn't look up.

"Sorry, I was helping Gladys get home. She sprained her ankle."

"No, we figured that part out. But look at you— Hey! Don't sit on my couch! The glitter!" Viv jumped up and retrieved several dishtowels, which she arranged on the couch.

"Some jerk-face practical joker filled the first aid kit with glitter. I was trying to find an ibuprofen for Gladys, and it spilled all over me."

Astrid spoke up. "Somebody really must have been messing with us then. They took all our staging directions and copies of the script too. They even took Riley's computer."

Emma turned back to Astrid. "Did you ever find them?"

"Yeah, we found them inside Caleb's backpack." Her eyes flicked toward one of the cast members Emma didn't know. He looked like a linebacker with a beard and baseball cap, but he had surprisingly delicate hands.

"I told you," he protested. "Riley asked me to hold on to them!"

"I think I would remember that," Riley muttered.

Emma swallowed a sip of her coffee and frowned. "Caleb, did you actually see Riley when they told you to collect the papers?"

"No… I was too busy helping Caesar—I mean Harold—with his toga."

"So it could have been someone who sounded like Riley."

Astrid looked to Riley. "What do you think, Professor? Fae? Wildling? Demon?"

"Ventriloquist? Clown? Stand-up comedian?" Riley continued.

"There *are* several mimics listed in the Seattle Lore Census…"

"Just because we study cryptids doesn't mean they're behind *everything*." They let out an exasperated sigh. "Does it even matter? Harold was murdered! I just can't believe Clarence did it. It seems so out of character."

"And he just stabbed him?"

"The actors all had fake knives. Like this," Astrid explained as she pulled a large steel dagger from her bag, handing it to Emma.

"It doesn't look fake. It's heavy. Looks like real metal too." The dagger glinted as she turned it in the light.

Astrid reached out until the tip of the blade touched her palm. She pushed. Instead of piercing her skin, the blade pushed harmlessly back into the handle. "It looks real, but it's a Halloween toy. I got them on clearance."

"So everyone used these prop knives except for Brutus— I mean Clarence? You'd think someone would have noticed."

Riley stared into the distance, fingering the top button of their shirt absentmindedly. "I just don't understand it. Clarence was really excited about this play."

"Maybe he was excited about killing Harold," Emma suggested. "It sounds like the man was awful."

"I understand what you all think of Clarence—that he's this bland little accountant who on weekends was the petty tyrant of the Neighborhood Association."

"Yeah, pretty much," Emma said. Everyone nodded.

"But I worked with him for months in rehearsal and… he was blossoming. He loved acting. When we started rehearsal, he seemed to be carrying a weight, but as time went on, the weight lifted."

"I'm sorry. I don't want to have to tell you this, but we

heard Clarence arguing with Harold right before the play. He threatened him."

"I still don't see it…" Riley shook their head. "Emma, you're a medium. Did you see Harold's departing spirit?"

"That's not really how it works." Emma shook her head. "Most people, when they die, they pass through the veil quickly. Some with unfinished business do get stuck here—"

"I know. So there's a chance that you could talk with him?"

"No. When people die traumatically, they're not able to talk for a while."

"Like, weeks? Months?"

"More like decades or centuries. They say it's like being scattered. It takes a long time for them to gather themselves."

"Meow." The captain stood and stretched. He hopped down from the coffee table, then jumped up into Emma's lap.

"Are you seeing this?" Emma asked Viv. "He never—"

Riley let out a moan. "But what are we going to *do*?"

"Do?" Emma said, sensing a trap. "What is there for us to do?"

"It just… seems like someone should look into this."

"I imagine the police will."

"If it was up to the police, an innocent man would be in prison right now for Jessie's murder."

"I don't understand what you want from me. We all saw Clarence kill Harold! That's nothing like what happened to Jessie."

"It's just not like Clarence to do something like that…"

"Normal, boring people do horrible things all the time!" Emma thought of Clarence and his picture-perfect wife.

"But what about the glitter? The voice that sounded like mine? The missing scripts? Doesn't it seem a little weird that those things would happen at the same time as a very unusual murder?"

"Maybe, but how is that my problem?"

"I just thought…"

"My problem is getting my water-damaged dining room somewhat usable before my mom and everyone I know show up for Thanksgiving dinner!"

"You did such a good job catching Jessie's killer—"

"My problem is going through a whole library of torn-up books so I can help Dash pass through the veil!"

Emma felt a hand on her shoulder. It was Viv. "Hey, Em, take a breath."

"And then when I get *all* that done, I can *finally* start applying for actual *jobs* so I can pull my *career* out of the tailspin it's in."

"Hey, Em, cool it for a minute. This is serious. Riley is asking for your help. When you needed our help with your investigation, we dropped everything even though we barely knew you. It's time for you to repay that favor."

"Come on, Viv." She bit her lip and looked away. Her hands twisted in front of her. She could feel everyone's eyes on her. "Fine."

"Fine?"

"Fine, I'll poke around a little. But I can't promise anything. I still think he did it."

Riley looked up. "Thanks, Emma."

CHAPTER 7
A CHORUS OF SHRIEKS

Back home, Emma collected her mail from the mailbox and walked up the front steps. Bills. Junk. The latest *Scientific American*. If she wasn't still a working scientist, she could at least read about them.

"Captain?" she called out, wondering if the cat had beaten her home. There was no answer.

Emma locked the door behind her, put her keys on the little hook by the door, and threw her purse onto a bench that doubled as a shoe rack. She kicked off her shoes and padded to the laundry room, where she changed her glitter-covered clothes into fresh ones from the basket. Then she ducked into the kitchen to put the magazine on top of the pile of magazines she would theoretically read one day. Settled, she went to the living room.

It always made her smile to enter that room. The living room was an oasis of calm in the middle of the house—wide and airy with high ceilings and tall windows that let in plenty of sun even on gray fall days.

A sofa upholstered in rich burgundy velvet faced a brick fireplace, a coffee table crafted from dark mahogany in front of it. On each side of the fireplace were two armchairs covered in a lush cream-colored fabric. An ornate Persian rug covered the hardwood floor from wall to wall.

She sank into the sofa. The soft cushions were warm from the light filtering through the windows. They embraced her like a favorite old blanket. Her plan, which she had made on the walk over, was to spend an hour by herself, staring at the wall. So many people had pulled her in so many directions for so long that she deserved to recharge.

But when her gaze inevitably fell upon the coffee table, she saw that her work wasn't over yet. A small stack of type-written pages lay before her. It was the captain's manuscript, and she'd promised him she'd read it weeks ago.

She sighed and grabbed the manuscript. Between the curiosity and her guilt from procrastination, there would be no chance of her properly relaxing until she read the story. So she read.

Sassy looked left and right. The circle of red eyes tightened. There was nothing to jump onto—no way of escape. He was facing everything the Sandpiper could throw at him, and he was going to do it alone.

That's right, he left me on a cliff-hanger last time. It had been only a few months ago, but it seemed like a lifetime. She continued reading.

Fur bristling, Sassy stood his ground. He didn't have any fear left—only anger. Anger at the Sandpiper, at Cheeto, and at the world in general.

Cheeto nodded. The rat took a step forward, raised its head, and let out a cry that sounded more like a scream. It was answered by a chorus of shrieks from the other rats.

Then the air was filled with flying fur and gnashing teeth. Sassy's vision was clouded by a fog of war. His claws flashed and teeth snapped. No matter how many rats he hit, it seemed like more came. He couldn't tell where one ended and the next began.

Sassy felt his vision blurring, and his legs gave out from under him. He collapsed onto the ground, and a cloud of rats fell on him, smothering him. He tried to fight back, but his body was too heavy to move.

Then as if in a dream, he heard the clarion call of a trumpet. Sassy felt himself being hoisted to his paws. A familiar scent greeted his nose. He looked up and saw the face of his savior.

"Colin?"

The cat looked into Sassy's eyes. "It's not over yet. Keep fighting."

Sassy felt new strength rising from the depths of his soul. He shook off the remnants of the rats' poison and turned to face the remaining vermin.

Colin walked beside him, his eyes never leaving the enemy. Together they turned to face the red-eyed horde.

"Just remember," Colin whispered from the corner of his mouth, "you're a lot stronger than you think."

Sassy nodded. He drew his claws and felt the blood pumping in his veins.

"Ready?" He turned toward Colin. "Then let's do this."

The two cats charged.

Emma marked up the manuscript, noting any typos and suggesting occasional improvements in sentence structure. Then she added a quick note of encouragement and stood.

She was going to return the papers to the captain's desk in his ornate study under the stairs, but when she got there, she found that light was seeping out from under the door and the distinctive *clacking* of his miniature typewriter filled the air.

Odd. She hadn't heard him come in the front.

She placed the pages on the floor next to the study,

weighting them down with the pen. Then she tiptoed back to the living room and threw herself on the sofa.

Finally! She unfocused her eyes and prepared to spend the rest of the hour doing absolutely nothing. It would be heaven. She closed her eyes, letting herself sink into the sofa. Then she heard a familiar voice.

"Hey, Emma, are you ready?"

CHAPTER 8
LIBRARY

Emma sat upright on the sofa and looked wearily at Dash, who had floated silently through the front door. He was standing in her living room, an expectant look on his face.

"Is it five o'clock already?" Looking at the spirit, she noticed he seemed a little droopier than usual. "Are you all right?"

"I'm okay. I was just thinking about what happened at the play. The world is an unusual place."

"You're telling me." She pulled a throw blanket off the couch and wrapped it around herself.

"I'm... deceased. Most of my friends are deceased. And yet, I don't believe I've ever seen anyone die before."

"Me neither. It surprised me that it looked just like part of the show. Why do you think Clarence did it? Riley said there's more going on than meets the eye."

"Isn't that always the case? People are hard to understand in the best of times."

"You're right. You know, I'm glad we have these little TV dates. It gets the mind off things like murderers and magic spells and missing bodies." She stood up and stretched, then slowly walked toward the TV room. "What's it going to be today? We're almost through season four of *Golden Girls*."

"Actually, I think I'd like to go to the library."

"Really? The library?"

"That was where you helped Alice pass through the veil, wasn't it?"

"Well… yeah, but I don't think the location was important."

"You said she passed through when you helped her remember—"

"I was only able to do that because I had her diary. We read it together."

"Emma, there's so much I don't remember. When I feel like I'm getting close, I blank out."

"But I don't have your diary."

"No, of course you don't. I'm not even sure I kept one. But I grew up here in Undertown. The library might have some record of me."

"Were you an author? I thought you were a law clerk when you were alive."

"I was part of a community. The community had a small local newspaper. I remember they ran the most mundane stories. There must be some mention of me."

"And you think the library might have copies of the news-paper in its archives."

"Precisely."

Emma rubbed the back of her neck as she searched for the right words. "Dash, have you been inside the library recently?"

———

"It's been destroyed!" Dash staggered backward.

"Definitely not by me. I mean, the library itself is in good shape, isn't it? Look at that light coming through those gorgeous stained-glass windows. Look at these beautiful desks—"

"But the books!" Dash gestured wildly to the floor, which was covered in pages torn from books. The pages were piled so thick a person nearly had to wade through them.

"The books... need a little work."

"You said that you did it? How?"

"I said I *didn't* do it. Alice did. Granted, I may have set her off with an insensitive question—"

"Insensitive?"

"She was in a vulnerable state. She may have... ripped the pages out of all the books and turned them into a creepy glowing tornado. Look, you just had to be there for it to make sense."

"There's no hope, is there?"

"Now don't start talking like that—"

"I'm never going to find out about my past and pass through the veil. I'm going to be stuck here for a thousand years!"

"You're catastrophizing, Dash."

"This is a catastrophe, Emma!"

"Hardly," she said, wading into the sea of pages. "Everything's still here. It's just a little... mixed up!" She bent over and picked up several pages. "Look, most of these are from the same book! We only need to sort them out."

"And how long will that take?"

"Oh, I don't know, five or six ye— It really depends on how many people we get to help! Oh, don't make that face."

"I'm not making a face."

"You are making a face. Look, here's an old newspaper. It's even an issue of the *Tattler* on top of the pile. 1922."

"Really?" Dash floated over to inspect it. "That's the last year I remember living."

"Let's take a look!" She reached down to pick up the old

newspaper, but when she tried to lift it, a big chunk of the paper tore away. "It's just kind of... brittle."

Tsk.

"What was that?" Emma said.

"Probably the sound of my heart breaking."

"Be quiet for a second."

Tsk.

"Very funny!" Emma called out. "You can come out now, Lily! I know you like to practice your haunting, but it's time to practice reading the room."

Tsk.

"Emma, I don't think that was Lily. I'd be able to sense her."

"Could it be Rue? Bob? Some other spirit I haven't met?"

"I... think we need to leave. Now."

CHAPTER 9
COLLECT CALL

"What the heck was that?" Emma asked, turning the dead bolt on her door.

"I don't know. I didn't see it."

"But you heard it?"

"Yes. I… I was frightened," said Dash.

"The dead guy was scared?"

"It's not something I'm accustomed to. It's rather… thrilling. But I have no desire to meet whatever that was."

"You're sure it couldn't have been another spirit like you?"

"Definitely not—we know our own kind. What I felt in there was entirely different."

"A sort of cold, hard indifference?" Emma asked.

"Yes. You felt it too."

A series of short buzzes emanated from Emma's pocket. She pulled her phone out and glanced at the screen. Her face fell.

Dash looked worried. "Who's calling?"

"A sort of cold, hard indifference," Emma sighed. "My mom."

"I thought you and your mom made up?" Dash said,

following Emma into the kitchen where she filled an electric kettle and turned it on.

"We did—kind of. We talked a lot on our road trip last summer. Turns out she had her reasons for being such an ice queen all my life."

"Well, that's progress."

"Maybe. Reasons or not, she's still an ice queen."

"Oh... I had thought she might have some insight on the veil."

"My mom?"

"She has the gift."

"She doesn't want it. She's spent the past forty years running from anything related to spirits, the paranormal, you name it."

"It is possible that she might have knowledge of these matters, even if she wishes to avoid contact with spirits like myself."

"I guess. You don't know her though. She's a living, breathing, human minefield. If I bring anything up too directly, she'll fly off the handle."

"I thought she worked through her feelings—"

"She barely admits to *having* feelings. I'll... figure it out though. Start by talking about the weather or something. I can bring up Aunt Cora. Maybe get her talking about the old days."

Emma's phone began to ring.

"No time like the present?" Dash offered.

"Fine. Let's get this over with." She answered the phone. "Hey, Mom. So wonderful to hear from you!"

But it wasn't her mom on the other end. "You have a collect call from inmate 12947 at King County Correctional Facility," said an automated message. "Press one to accept charges."

"Ms. Day, I'm so glad I was able to catch you. This is Clarence."

Emma found, in that moment, that she didn't know what you were supposed to say when somebody you barely knew and didn't really like called you collect from jail. "Umm… uhhh," she stammered.

"I suppose you're wondering why I've called you."

"That is a fair assumption. Yeah, let's start there."

"Well, I'm in a bit of a pickle. I've been arrested for murdering Harold."

"I was there."

"Oh dear. This is so embarrassing. Of course in ten years, we'll probably look back on all this and laugh."

"In… ten years? When you get out of jail?"

"Why would I be in jail for ten years?"

"Because you *killed Harold Loftus!* You did it in front of everyone! I'm not sure what you think you're doing calling me, but I don't usually talk with killers—"

"No, you don't believe I'm guilty, do you? We had such a good rapport."

"Rapport? I lost my house because of you! And again, yes, I literally saw you stab the man."

"I'm afraid we've had a bit of a miscommunication."

"Oh really? Didn't you vote to kick me out of the neighborhood?"

"No, I didn't. The Neighborhood Association voted to. I voted to let you stay—argued in favor of it in fact."

"You… did?"

"Of course I did! That was one of the most spectacular meetings we've ever had. They accused you of murder, but then you turned it around and exposed the true killer! Magnificent work. I couldn't have done it better myself."

"You know I can find out if you're lying."

"Of course. I know the kinds of powers you have access to. As you said, you are Emma Barrow, niece of Coralee Barrow. That's why I assumed you would know that I'm innocent."

Emma sighed. "Fine… I'll assume for the moment you're telling the truth. How could you be innocent when I saw you stab the victim?"

"It was the knife. Someone exchanged my prop knife with a real one."

"That's a pretty thin excuse."

"It doesn't matter, because it happens to be the truth."

"Then tell me why. Why would anyone want Harold dead? Why would they want to have you take the fall?"

"Undertown, like the world around it, is more complicated than you could imagine—"

"You have one minute remaining in this call…"

"I don't have much time. Talk with Darla from the Neighborhood Association. She's on the good side—"

"Your call has ended."

"Well, that was intense," Emma said to herself before remembering that Dash was in the room. "Clarence says he's innocent. He wants my help."

"So his story was believable?"

"No, it was absurd—so absurd I'm actually tempted to believe him." Emma stared absently into the distance until the sound of the cat door broke her reverie.

A moment later, the captain padded in. Emma bent over to pet him, but the moment he sniffed her, he recoiled. He shook himself, then circled around her, sniffing.

"What's the matter? Smell a rat?" She tried sniffing, but whatever the captain sensed was too subtle for her underpowered human nose to detect.

"Look at the way his fur is standing on end."

"What's the matter, Captain?" Emma said, bending over again to try to pet him.

He hissed. Then his green-and-yellow eyes narrowed into a steely glare. He rushed outside through the cat door.

Dash circled Emma. "I wonder what he detected on your clothes."

"Could you stop? Maybe he overheard us and ran off to solve the murder. That would be great, actually. Then I can finally have time to finish patching my walls and learn to make turkey before Thanksgiving."

"I… think I'm going to follow him and see what's brewing."

"That would be a juicy tidbit for your gossip club: *Captain Leaps out of Retirement!*"

Dash laughed. "The thought *did* occur to me." He began floating away, then looked back over his shoulder. "Don't forget to call your mother."

"Mother. Yeah. Right away."

Emma unlocked her phone and pulled up her mom's number. She stared at the screen, thumb poised above the dial button, until the phone fell back asleep. Then she put it away.

"Now… I wonder where to find Darla."

CHAPTER 10
STRANGER IN A BROWN SUIT

Darla was, like Gladys, one of the board members of the Undertown Neighborhood Association. Until now, her chief role in Emma's life had consisted of shoving unwanted microphones in her face and delivering bad news.

Emma had no idea where to find her short of setting up an ambush at the next board meeting. Luckily, she knew some people who did. Spirits, to be more precise.

The rain had picked up, and the sidewalk was slick as she turned the corner that led to the Ghost Hunters' Club.

Note the apostrophe: Hunters'.

If this organization had been called the Ghost Hunters Club, then one might conclude that this was a club for people who hunted ghosts. That would be a mistake because this club was for ghosts who hunted people.

Rather, they hunted people's dirty laundry, malapropisms, scandals, and fire takes. In a word, they hunted gossip—the perfect hobby for a group of spirits who could pass through walls and had infinite time to kill.

If anyone would know about Darla, it would be them.

Their clubhouse was in the boarded-up office of a former

travel agency located only a few blocks away from Emma's house. In fact, it was right around the next corner—

"Excuse me, miss."

Emma did a double take. The man who approached her looked like a 1962 Sears catalog come to life. He wore a dull brown suit with a stubby red tie and brown felt hat. Thick, tortoise-shell glasses completed the look.

"Are you the owner?"

"The owner?"

"Of this building. I'm attempting to find them."

"No… I'm not the owner." Emma looked at the man, trying to figure out if she'd seen him before, but she drew a blank. "I'm not sure who is."

"It just looked like you were walking here."

"I'm not sure how you could know that." It wasn't technically a lie. Unconsciously, she gripped her bag tighter to her body.

"Just a hunch. Thought I'd get lucky, and you'd save me the trouble of digging through the records."

"Why, exactly, are you looking for the owner of this building?"

"I'm not entirely sure. My employer simply gave me a list and dropped me off." He held up a clipboard that held a stack of pages. The paper was pink and flimsy like the reverse of a carbon copy. "I'd be careful if I were you, miss. It looks like people have been in here. Could be squatters. I… uh, looked in the window."

"And if there were, what would happen to them when you finish your work and give the information to your employer?"

He looked puzzled. "Hadn't considered that. It's really none of my business."

"So who is your client exactly?"

He flashed a grin. "Strictly confidential. But between you and me, you can't expect a large block of real estate to become available in a major city without certain people sitting up and taking notice. What was your name again?"

"Emma."

"Ah, yes. I love what you've done with your house by the way. As much as I've loved our little chat, I really should get back to it. Nose to the grindstone." The man walked away, whistling a Benny Goodman tune. Emma could still hear him after he turned the corner.

"Is he gone, dear?" It was Rue, who looked worried. Behind her were Bob and Lily, all members of the gossip-hunting club.

"I... think so?"

"He came in through the window."

"What? He said he only looked through the window!"

"And he made quite a mess, riffling through the research materials that you set out for us to read. We all got out."

"Aren't you spirits? Nobody can see you," Emma said.

"He had a strange energy. It... frightened us."

"Yeah, I felt it too. The way he dressed. The way he acted. He's looking for the owner of the building—I guess this part of town was abandoned for so long the old owners are hard to track down."

"They want to buy the clubhouse and kick us out," Rue said.

Emma considered that. "Do you really think so?"

"It's what businessmen do, dear." Rue looked away bitterly. "I've seen their kind at work. They're sharks, and all these empty buildings are blood in the water."

"Then we'll haunt the bastards!" Bob shouted, looking not unlike an angry garden gnome.

"I've been practicing my haunting," Lily offered, glowing ethereally as if to prove a point.

"No, dears," said Rue. "That wouldn't do us any good. One doesn't want to have to haunt one's own house." She shook her head. "No, we'll have to move. This world is for the living, after all."

"Hey," Emma said, "don't give up just yet. I'm sure we can find a way to help you keep the clubhouse. Do any of you know who owns this place? Maybe we can convince them not to sell?"

"I have no clue," Rue said. The others shook their heads.

"Well, I'll just have to figure it out then. But right now I need your help with something else. I need to know about Darla from the Neighborhood Association."

"Darla?" Rue tapped a spectral finger against her lip. "What do we know about Darla? Twice divorced. Husbands both married her for money, and she kicked them to the curb when it became apparent. I like her, though like most people, she's become a bit dull with age."

"Do you know where she lives?"

"Oh certainly. She lives on Easthill."

CHAPTER 11
HILL HOUSE

The historical geography of Undertown was so peculiar that it could fill up several volumes. However, such books were hard to come by, as the authors kept getting lost.

Like most of life, it used to be simpler. The core and its vibrant, tree-lined Undertown Square were once the most prosperous parts of the neighborhood. The outskirts were rougher.

The curse changed all that. Residents of the core fled outward. They renamed Perimeter Road to Main Street and filled it with shops and apartments. They built houses on the tree-lined hills that cradled Undertown and separated it from greater Seattle.

The nicest houses were on Easthill. The nicest of the nicest were at its top.

Emma stood at the bottom of Easthill. Far above her, picture windows reflected the last rays of the setting sun. She considered the steep staircase that would take her up the forested hill, through the firs and hemlocks, to Darla's house.

How long could it take to climb?

———

The answer, Emma discovered, was that it could take a very long time. Especially with the autumn night falling like a curtain.

Something touched her shoulder, and she slapped it. A maple's twiggy finger dragged across her skin, then suddenly sprang behind her. Its sudden noise startled an unseen creature, which bolted—hopefully away.

Just when it seemed like she'd never reach the top, she did. There was a post with a brass placard that said THE MILLERS. Next to it, a flagstone path led to a door.

It was a very expensive-looking door. A large oval window in the center held a stained-glass depiction of a ship on stormy seas. Next to it was a brass knocker in the shape of a lion's head.

She knocked. There was movement on the other side. The door cracked open, and a wary eye examined her. Then the sound of a chain unlatching.

"Emma Day?" Darla said, opening the door. "You're not who I expected."

———

"One lump or two?" Darla said, pouring mint tea from a clear tea press into a bone china cup that sat in front of Emma.

"Two, thanks." Emma watched Darla use a pair of tiny tongs to select two irregular lumps of sugar from a bowl and drop them into her cup.

"I always wondered. Do they carve the lumps of sugar from sugar cubes? Do they use molds? The kinds of things an old woman thinks about."

"I… don't know how they do it. I like them though. They're cute." She stirred her tea to help the sugar dissolve. "You've got an amazing view up here."

"You'd think I'd get tired of it after forty years in this house..." Her voice trailed off as she took in the view from the large picture window next to them.

On Main Street, far below, you could only see people's shadows as they waded through pools of light from the streetlamps. In the distance, the houses of Westhill looked like a sky full of stars.

"When Henry and I came up here, the hill was mostly pine and fir. We had to hire a team of lumberjacks to clear the site and hoist the trees away."

"You moved here from the core?"

"We did. Though nobody called it the core then. But you didn't come to talk to an old lady about the past."

"Clarence called me. He asked me for help—said to talk to you."

"Nobody who really knows him thinks he could have murdered Harold. He's the Neighborhood Association's resident bleeding heart. Oh, that's an unfortunate turn of phrase."

"So he didn't vote to take away the house I'd inherited?"

"No. Neither did I, for that matter. It's darned useful to have a Barrow woman around."

"But the hearing seemed so bureaucratic and impersonal."

"The word you're looking for is *efficient*. Look, honey, some of us have been on that board longer than you've been alive. What are you? Twenty-five? Twenty-six?"

"I'm... just going to let you believe that."

"Regardless, each member of the board knows where they stand. We know our deal breakers. We know what's negotiable. So we're efficient. Sometimes the chips fall your way, and sometimes they don't."

"That sounds frustrating."

"Oh, it is. Makes it hard to ram things through, but to some of us, that's the point. Of course you already know that." She winked.

"What do I already know?" Emma sighed and set her tea on the table too hard. "Clarence said the same thing. He expected me to know he was innocent right away."

"You don't... Oh my. Didn't Cora teach you anything?"

"No! I barely remember meeting the woman."

"Well, that certainly changes things. You must understand that the Neighborhood Association isn't as useless as it seems. We don't just fill potholes. Our main purpose is to maintain the delicate balance between Undertown and the outside world."

"You want to keep people out."

"No, we don't, though I understand why you might think that." Darla smiled and shook her head. "We keep things balanced. What do you know about magic?"

"What... do *you* know about magic?"

"Touché!" Darla chuckled. "The answer is not much. None of us really do, but we know that there's something about this neighborhood that attracts it."

"Aunt Cora helped you fight it off."

"She helped keep it in balance."

"You know"—Emma bit her lip—"she was the one who made the core unlivable. She tried to work a spell, and it backfired."

"We wouldn't be very good administrators if we didn't know that. Clarence especially knows where the cards lie. That's why he called you."

"What?"

"Even if Cora didn't teach you a thing, you have her books, her notes, and her blood. There are lots of... things that would love to come in and take advantage of our neighborhood. What better way than to discredit the Neighborhood Association?"

"By framing Clarence for murder! So perhaps the killer wasn't after Harold Loftus at all. He was just a convenient victim to set up Clarence."

"It's possible. I don't know of anyone who would want Harold dead. He spent most of his time at work. No family. No close ties. I only know this from casual observations. We weren't in the same social circles."

"So... where do I start? I might be the only one who can help, but I'm still new to town. I only know a few people."

Darla bit her bottom lip and looked out the window for a moment before turning to Emma. "I would start by talking with our chief social worker, Marcus Walker. He's the neighborhood liaison with the county sheriff. He would have handled the crime scene. I'll call him and let him know to expect you."

"Thanks."

"I would also look into Clarence's wife, Clarice."

"Clarence and... Clarice?"

"I know. Too cute by half. Still, they've had a rough patch. She's been making unusual trips around town."

"How do you know that?"

Darla merely gestured to a telescope next to the large window. It wasn't pointed at the stars.

"Hold on, dear, you've got something—" Darla reached over to Emma's sweater and pulled off a small shiny speck.

"I thought I got it all off! Somebody filled the community center's first aid kit with glitter. I was helping Gladys, and it exploded on me."

"What happened to Gladys?"

"She twisted her ankle."

Darla snorted. "Maybe it will keep her off my back. Still, I suppose I'll be a good neighbor and send flowers."

———

The walk down the hill was easier than Emma expected and not nearly as treacherous as she feared. Lights were embedded in the walkway, and the timer had switched on while Emma was with Darla.

She was still mulling over the conversation when she arrived in front of Deadtown. So the Neighborhood Association was more than it appeared. They knew about magic, for one thing. They knew that Cora and Diedre caused the problem with the core, though they didn't seem to know exactly how any of it worked.

Now it made a lot more sense as to why Clarence would call her, specifically, to ask for help. She was from a family that dealt with unseen forces, with the paranormal, with magic... Too bad her only mystic power was watching daytime TV with her friend who died a hundred years ago.

And she still needed to call her mom. *Ugh.*

"Hey, Em." Viv greeted her from behind a howling milk frother. She turned a knob, quieting the machine. Viv poured the foam into a ceramic cup, then artfully poured in espresso to create a pattern in the foam. She slid the finished drink to a waiting customer.

"Hey, Viv, you seen Riley around? I need to talk with them about the case."

"I guess that means you're on board?"

Emma shrugged. "This town has a way of sucking me in."

"They're in the back. Riley and the crew needed somewhere private to meet. I'm sure they won't mind us saying hi." Viv finished wiping the counter with a white towel, then flipped the towel over her shoulder. "Come on."

The entry into the back office was covered by a curtain. It was small, just a desk and chair next to a ratty sofa. Boxes of cups, napkins, plastic utensils, unsold T-shirts, and other merchandise lined the walls and reached up to the dusty acoustic-tile ceiling.

At the far side of the room, a group of five people were engaged in a serious conversation. "We *have* to cancel the show. How could we not after something like this?"

"*We* didn't kill anybody. Why should *we* have to shut down the troupe?"

"I didn't say we would shut down, just press Pause and let things cool off."

"Y'all are forgetting that we raised a ton of money at that show. The people in this neighborhood want us to fix up the old theater. If we don't do that, it'll be like we stole their money."

"Hey, guys," Viv said, waving her hand. Five worried faces looked up at her.

"Oh hey, Viv. Hey, Emma," Riley said. "We were just figuring out what to do next."

"It's a tricky situation," Emma said.

"Tell me about it. How's the, uh, investigation?"

"I haven't found anything concrete, but I'm starting to think you might be right. Clarence could be innocent."

"Oh?"

Emma paused, considering her words. "He called me from jail. Said that someone swapped out his prop knife with a real one."

"That makes perfect sense in light of our own research."

"Research?"

"Into the pranks we've been experiencing. The missing scripts. The misplaced computer—"

"Don't forget the glitter bomb."

"We haven't. We've cataloged it along with dozens of other examples beginning two days ago and occurring within a tight geographical radius."

"Are you implying that the prankster could be the murderer?"

"If Clarence told you that his prop knife was replaced with a real one, it matches the pattern."

"It does seem to match, but what kind of person would *do* that? I'm not even sure how it would be possible to pull dozens of pranks without being discovered."

"Unless it isn't a person at all."

"I don't like where this is going, Riley."

"Tell me, Emma, have you ever heard of the Waterloo demon?"

CHAPTER 12
DEMONOLOGY

Emma sat hunched over, holding her head in her hands.

"I first began to suspect that something unusual was afoot when our scripts went missing. I knew it sounded like a piece of lore, but I couldn't quite put my finger on it."

Emma moaned, "My mom thinks everything is a fricking demon. I am so sick of hearing about demons."

"Precisely. Demonology as a subfield of practical folklore is, frankly, looked down upon. Too much overlap with religion, at least in the West. I admit I'm not immune. It was Astrid who found the connection."

"It was simple once I understood what to look for," Astrid said. "Forget the religious overtones. Demons are like tornadoes of emotion and compulsion."

"The compulsion to play practical jokes?" Emma asked.

"More like the compulsion to put things where they don't belong."

"That seems so benign though."

Riley leaned in. "Until you learn the real reason Napoleon lost Waterloo: he couldn't find the map."

"That's ridiculous," Emma said, then hesitated. "Isn't it?"

"If you examine the primary sources, you'll find dozens of mix-ups like that. People have speculated that it was due to demonic activity."

"And that the Duke of Wellington actually summoned the demon."

Emma frowned and sat upright. "A demon that puts things where they don't belong, huh? That would make it a kind of... entropy demon."

"A chaos demon," Riley said. "Fortunately, I happen to know someone who knows about chaos demons."

"That's great."

"Not exactly. I might have... gotten her fired."

———

Emma stared at the lights of the Space Needle from the back seat of Riley's Prius. She couldn't help but feel a thrill of excitement, being on an adventure into greater Seattle with her friends on this dark, drizzly night.

"So what's the plan?" Emma asked.

"I... don't really know. Show up and hope she's forgiven me? It wasn't really *my* fault."

"You said you got her fired."

"Yeah, but technically, *she* was the one who falsified her research. I just pointed it out—"

"Oof."

"—to the dean."

"Yeah, we're doomed. It's nice to get out and see the sights though," Emma said, looking out the window. Lights from distant container ships streaked the dark water of Puget Sound.

"You haven't had much of a chance to explore Seattle yet, have you?" Riley asked.

"No, I've been so busy with my house." They turned onto a street filled with bars and restaurants, then began climbing an incredibly steep hill.

"Undertown isn't the only… unique place around here."

"It's not?"

The top of the hill was filled with shops that sold small, precious things.

"I'll have to take you to the night market sometime. We'll go say hi to the kraken— Ooh, I bet you'd love the floating book fair," Riley said, stopping the car in front of an enormous house with an impeccably manicured yard.

"The… what?"

"Well, this is the place. I bet we can convince Mallory to see reason."

———

"Absolutely not."

"Mallory, I know you're upset with me—"

"Upset with you? Why would I be upset with you? I love being an adjunct at Pacific Community College."

"Oof, you work for Pacific now? That place is awful."

"Well, there're not a lot of jobs out there for someone who was fired from her *tenure track* position at U-Dub. You ruined my life, Riley."

"Me? I wasn't the one *making things up* and passing them off as legitimate research! What was I supposed to do?"

"You were supposed to give me a little freaking *sympathy!*"

"Why—?"

"I thought you of all people would understand. It's inhumane how much work they expect us to do. Publish or perish, right?"

"That's just how the system works," Riley said.

"So when Michael died, and I could barely drag myself out of bed for months, I was just supposed to perish?"

"I... didn't know."

"You didn't ask. I did make up some data, yeah. It was that or lose everything I'd worked for. But I was always going come back and fix it. To publish a retraction once I got my life in order. You never gave me that chance."

"God, I feel like such a jerk." Riley looked stunned. "I'm sorry."

"What do you want?"

"Your expertise."

Mallory snorted. "I haven't heard that in a while."

"You always were the expert on demons. We have possible demonic activity on our hands."

"This just keeps getting better and better. Didn't you tell me that my work on demons—what were your words?— smelled more like religion than science?"

"I... might have said that. I was wrong."

"Well, which one is it?"

"Waterloo."

"Nice. How do you know that I didn't summon it to teach you a lesson?"

"Did you?"

"I wish I had that kind of money. I spend everything I have trying to keep this house from falling apart," Mallory spat out.

"Maybe... we could make a deal?"

"Out with it."

"You help me out, and I'll include you as a coauthor on any journal articles that result from this work. That will help you if you ever want to apply for a research position again."

Mallory was silent for a moment, then spoke. "I want to be second author."

"I can't do that. It wouldn't be fair to Astrid. She's been working night and day."

"You always were loyal to your students. I do respect that. I'll take third author."

"Agreed."

"Now why don't you come in off my porch and get this over with?" Mallory ushered them in. "Take off your shoes."

The inside of the house was like a museum. The hall was lined with glass cases, each one displaying a different artifact: a stone tablet with a carving of a snake, a gold coin with the profile of a woman's face, and an enormous black feather.

The professor ushered everyone to a dining room. In the center sat an enormous oak table covered in maps, charts, and books.

"It looks like you've been doing research on your own time."

"There's always work for... skilled consultants. Sit. Don't touch anything. Now, what do you want to know?"

"What do you know about the Waterloo demon?"

"I know that its name, Waterloo demon, is Eurocentric. It's been reported at many battles and historic failures throughout the world. Other than that, it's a pure chaos demon. Blows through like a hurricane."

"How is it summoned?"

"Nobody knows, though it sounds like someone might have figured it out. All we know for sure is that it requires destroying a large quantity of gold. They're only summoned for matters of great importance."

"Detection?"

"I don't believe any modern practitioner of applied folklore has ever encountered it, so it's all guesswork, but I believe Mansard et al. published a hypothetical study. He hypothesized that demonic entities of entropic genus should all leak chaos, and therefore they should be detectable in any of their forms if you had the right instrument."

"A kind of... demonic Geiger counter?"

"Precisely. It's feasible for both positive and negative delta entropic demons."

Emma leaned forward, "Excuse me. You mentioned summoning. I was wondering how to make the thing leave."

Mallory's laugh had an edge to it that sent a shiver down Emma's spine. "How do you make a hurricane leave? You don't."

CHAPTER 13
WAFFLE

"And what'll it be for you, darlin'?" The waitress popped her bubblegum.

"The waffle breakfast," Emma replied.

"Eggs?"

"Over easy." The waitress walked off. "I was beginning to forget what a political, cutthroat place academia can be," Emma said to Riley, folding her menu and putting it away.

"Tell me about it. I hope I didn't make a huge mistake trusting her."

"She seemed sincere."

"But she's known to have published fraudulent data. I just hope having her listed as a collaborator won't cast a shadow over the work. Still, we got a solid lead."

Emma laughed. "Talk about casting a shadow. If my old boss in the chemistry department saw me here talking openly about literal demons, he'd have a heart attack."

"That's what's the food's for," quipped Astrid.

Emma sipped her coffee and smiled. She hadn't been out to a late-night diner with friends since, well, her undergrad days. It was nice.

She looked around the diner with its chrome tables and

red vinyl booths and its odd assortment of aging jocks, punks, and goths.

She turned back to her friends. "So this demon. What does it look like? Fangs and bat wings?"

"Maybe, maybe not," Riley said.

"They take whatever form suits them," Astrid added. "They can also mimic voices and sounds."

"So anyone could be a demon? How are you supposed to find them?"

"They can sometimes be spotted by their outdated clothing and mannerisms," Riley said.

"They don't get out much," Astrid agreed. "Society can change a lot in a hundred years. Heck, even fifty years."

"All right," the waitress said, approaching them with three large plates. "We've got a Tillicum slam, a waffle, and a biscuits and gravy. Anything else? No? Enjoy then."

Emma grinned at the steaming waffle in front of her. She picked up the tiny white jug of syrup and dumped it on top, careful to avoid the fresh strawberries and blueberries that lined the plate.

The waffle was crisp on the outside, light and airy inside. The warm maple syrup added a complex sweetness, and the salty butter added a depth of flavor that was nothing short of perfection. She opened her eyes and looked around the table.

The recent conversation played back through Emma's mind: *whatever form suits them... outdated clothing...* Her fork fell from her fingers and clattered to the plate. The others looked up from their food. "The man in the brown suit!"

CHAPTER 14
CAT DOOR

Emma got home after midnight. She closed the door and looked out the front window. She could see Riley and Astrid's flashlight beams disappearing into the darkness.

They still hadn't gotten the streetlights working in the core. The original lampposts were there. They had electricity. But the bulbs were of a make that could only be found in museums, and the museums didn't want to share.

It was good of them to walk her home. She never minded living alone, but with all the talk of demons—of the man in the brown suit possibly *being* a demon—walking home alone would not have been fun.

She flicked on the light and saw a face looking at her.

"Did you wait up for me?" she asked the captain, who was sitting on a bench in the hallway. The captain merely yawned in reply.

"I'm pretty tired myself. I think I'll turn in." Emma took off her shoes and walked upstairs to her bedroom, where she slipped out of her day clothes and into a silky nightgown.

The evening had seemed like a dream. She'd been whisked away into Riley's world—a world where people talked about summoning demons in the precise, analytical language of academia.

In the moment, it had all seemed so real. But now, back at home, washing her face, climbing into bed, it seemed so implausible.

She picked up her book, *Death on the Nile,* and started to read as the night's rain began in earnest. Soon the book fell from her hands. She fell asleep to the sound of raindrops and woke up to chaos.

"Yowl!"

Emma shot upright. *Something's moving downstairs.* She turned on the lamp, swung her legs out of bed, and opened her nightstand drawer. Without taking her eyes from the door, she reached into the open drawer until her fingers found the cold, hard metal object she expected: bear spray.

She stood, tiptoed around the squeakiest board in her floor, and pressed her ear to the door. The sound of something hard and metallic hitting the floor sent a shiver down her spine and shocked her into action.

She opened the door and rushed to the stairwell. In the darkness below, she saw a pair of eyes flash.

Heart racing, she flicked on the light, holding the canister of bear spray in front of her as she waited for her vision to adjust.

As it did, she saw a pair of eyes, one brown and one yellow, staring up from the darkness.

"Captain?" Emma lowered the enormous canister of pepper spray and tentatively stepped downstairs.

The formidable feline turned away from her and faced the front door, hair standing on end as if he expected something to attack him at any moment.

Around him, the room looked like a tornado had passed through. Coats and shoes lay scattered around the floor. The rustic tin umbrella holder she'd thrifted had been thrown to the opposite end of the hallway, and it looked like it had knocked a framed photo of Emma's mother off the wall when it hit.

"What happened, Captain?" She waited for a reply though she knew none would come. "This would be a lot easier if you could talk *and* type. Maybe you could write me a letter?"

The captain ignored her.

"That must be a pretty interesting cat door with the way you're staring at it." She bent over to inspect it more closely and noticed a tuft of black-and-brown hair stuck in its hinge. "Oh… I get it. Did the cat door bite you? Pull your hair? That would have freaked me out too."

"Mrow." The captain looked defiantly up at her.

"It's okay. Nothing looks broken," she said, picking up a jacket and hanging it on the coat stand. "You're just a little on edge today. A murder will do that, I suppose. And with all the talk of demons… Let's have a snack and try to forget about it."

Emma finished tidying and began walking back to the kitchen.

"Oh, come on." She called back to the captain, who was still eyeing the door warily. "I'll look at the cat door later today. It's not going to come after you."

Reluctantly, the captain followed her into the kitchen. Emma opened the refrigerator, pulled out a small jug of cream, and poured some into a bowl, which she put on the floor. A bagel went into the toaster for herself.

The bagels were a new treat. Since that annoying Chef Jack moved into her aunt's old house, he had branched out from croissants and begun offering a wider variety of baked goods. The croissants were still the best thing on the menu, but sometimes a girl wanted a bagel.

The toaster sprang the bagel upward, filling the air with the scent of freshly toasted bread. Emma carefully extracted it and topped it with thick, white mascarpone cheese and the ruby-red raspberry preserves that had been a gift from

Diedre. She carried it to the breakfast table, sat down, and bit in.

The way the warm bagel contrasted with the cool, creamy mascarpone was heaven. The sticky sweet-and-sour raspberries sent a pleasant shiver down her spine. She finished the bagel, washing it down with a sip of milk, and glanced over to her phone, which was charging on the counter. It was five in the morning.

Was it worth trying to go back to sleep? The sun wouldn't rise until seven, but she knew from experience that if she woke up after four, sleep was a lost cause.

It wasn't so bad; she liked quiet mornings with the house to herself. She made a cup of black tea and walked back through the hall into her living room. On a chair by the darkened front window was a copy of Agatha Christie's *The Moving Finger* with a tasseled bookmark at the halfway point.

Emma set her tea on the side table, sat down, and opened the book, pulling out the cloth bookmark that had been woven like a Persian rug. She pulled her feet up onto the chair and began to read. A weight fell off her shoulders as she relaxed and enjoyed the moment to herself.

In the kitchen, the phone began to ring.

CHAPTER 15
FACETIME

Who on earth could be calling me at five in the morning? Emma reluctantly slid the bookmark back into her book, placed it on the side table, and got up from her comfy chair.

She knew of course. There was only one person who would ever call her so early. In the kitchen, she unplugged her phone, glanced at the lock screen, and sighed. She took the call.

"Hi, Mom. Did you know you can still just call? You don't have to FaceTime."

"That's all right. I like to see your face, dear. And why are you dressed like you just pulled yourself out of bed?"

"There's a little thing we need to talk about. It's called time zones. It's literally five o'clock here."

"The early bird catches the worm. Shouldn't you be getting ready for work?"

"I'm a chemistry professor—a lazy intellectual. We sleep in."

"Thank goodness. For a moment, I thought you were still unemployed." The woman really knew where to stick the knife in.

"Not that it's any of your business, but the captain—I mean the cat—woke me up. Something's wrong with the cat door."

"Can't you lock it at night?"

Emma glance at the captain, who had finished his cream and was walking purposefully back to the hall. "I don't think he'd like that." She took another bite of bagel. "So why are you calling at five a.m.?"

"I… had a feeling something might have happened up there. I just wanted to check in and make sure you're safe."

"A feeling? Really."

"If you ever get around to giving me grandbabies, Emma Day, you'll find out you don't stop worrying about your children even when they've grown."

"Are you sure one of your spirit guides didn't whisper something in your ear?"

"You know I don't consort with demons."

"I know you try to make yourself look squeaky clean compared with Aunt Cora. But I know you have the gift too."

"The gift. That's what Coralee called it. And you picked it up and start repeating it to me like you know what you're talking about. I guess I shouldn't complain. I did raise you to be headstrong."

"What exactly did they tell you happened? Why were you worried?"

The voice on the other end was silent for so long that Emma began to worry that the call had dropped. Then her mother spoke. "Emma, do you know what the gift really is?"

"I don't know. It means you can see dead people? See spirit guides? See weird creepy women in dirty wedding dresses?"

"Oh my—you saw her?"

"A few months ago. She was there when I found Alice Beyer's diary. Why? Who is she?"

"We used to call her Miss Havisham. That's not her real

name. It's what we called her. Cora thought she was a spirit guide. I thought she was…"

"A demon."

"Well, yes. You would too if she came to you when you were twelve years old, at night, alone, whispering secrets that no child should ever have to hold on to." The woman let out a long sigh, and her voice grew wearier. "The gift."

The sudden display of vulnerability took Emma off guard, and she was silent.

Her mom continued, "The gift of the fae. It sounds nice when you say it like that. It sounds like something from a fairy tale, that you of all little girls would be picked to live a magical life." The woman let out a bitter laugh. "But the fae don't give gifts. They make deals."

"Mom, what are you talking about?" Emma struggled to take in this sudden deluge of information.

"Three hundred years ago, Alistair Barrow took his first-born daughter and walked out of his English village to the crossroads. There he made a deal with… something. I've spent my whole life trying to get out of that bargain—trying to get you out."

"You're saying there's a price? What could it be?"

"The gift of the fae is the curse of knowledge. Being in contact with things like Miss Havisham—it changes you."

"You mean she's not just another wandering spirit?"

"Oh no, she's much older. Less human. But even the human spirits will change you. They think that just because you can see them, you can help them. They'll stick on you like leeches and suck you dry."

"You mean there's not a way to help them?"

"I know you've never liked me to talk about evil. It doesn't fit in that scientific brain of yours. So you write it off and say I'm a silly old woman. But evil exists, Emma. Sometimes the best you can do is protect yourself."

———

Well, that was a bummer.

Emma put away her phone and picked up the captain's dish to rinse it. The cat wasn't in the kitchen or the hall or the living room. *He must have risked the cat door,* she thought.

She drew the blinds and looked out the curved front window onto the large park in the middle of Undertown Square. It had begun to fill with a soft, aimless light that rolled in like a fog.

The fae don't give gifts... What does that even mean?

She walked to the chair from earlier, sat, and picked up her Miss Marple book, absentmindedly opening it and resting her unfocused eyes on the page.

Alistair Barrow made a bargain... with the fae? With a demon?

Her stomach felt sour, and her vision began to swim as the implications of these new facts swirled through her mind. But at the center of her chest, she felt a hot anger rising.

It didn't matter if it was three hundred years ago or yesterday. Yet another mediocre man had screwed something up, gotten in over his head, and left Emma holding the bill. She let this familiar flame of anger grow and used its light to find her way back to the present.

Bam! She jumped at the sound and looked down, surprised to find that she'd slammed her book closed. She remembered her plan.

She was going to track down Marcus Walker, the person who Darla said was the liaison between the neighborhood and the county sheriff. Then she needed to look into Clarence's marriage to see if it was as shaky as it was made out to be. Finally, there was the demon angle. She'd ask around about the man in the brown suit.

She went upstairs and changed into skinny jeans, a blouse, a Patagonia puffer, and Merrill hiking shoes.

Demons? Fae? Spirits? They could move or get run over. Emma was on the case.

CHAPTER 16
VINYL

Tiny droplets of water misted Emma's face as she crossed Undertown Square. She double-checked the address for Marcus Walker's office, hoping it was at street level. After her early wake-up, the last thing she wanted was to climb more stairs.

To her left was the old theater with its peeling paint and darkened windows. She'd never admit it to Riley, but it seemed like it would be an impossible task for their little band of amateur actors to restore such an imposing building.

Even restoring the intricately decorated facade would be a challenge. The front was covered in tile that depicted trees and vines in relief. They snaked up the walls, around sculpted columns, past the marquee, all the way up to the roof where those two gargoyles—

Hold on—where did the other gargoyle go? Fear's icy finger ran up Emma's spine. She pushed it down. She had things to do.

Evil exists.

No. Whatever she had seen the other day was obviously her imagination. Gargoyles were stone. They did not wink. If they did, it would be impossible to see from such a distance.

As she walked the rest of the way to the social worker's office, she was *totally fine*. She was *not worried at all*. If anything, she was the picture of a *calm, collected scientist.*

She arrived not at an office but at a house—a pale yellow stucco with green shutters. The front door was painted green and had a small window inset at the top. Beside it a green metal mailbox was attached to the wall. The name WALKER was spelled out in reflective stick-on letters.

Emma knocked on the door and waited. A curtain in the window fluttered, and a moment later, the door opened to reveal an elderly Black woman.

She stared at Emma for a moment before recognition lit up her face. "You must be Emma. I heard all about you. Come on in." She ushered Emma inside and closed the door behind her. "Marcus will be out in a minute. I just put some tea on to boil. Like a cup? Sit down."

"I'd love a cup." Emma sat on the olive-green couch which was enrobed in a clear vinyl slipcover. A moment later, the woman returned and sat on the chair across from Emma, placing two steaming mugs on the coffee table. She took her mug and sipped. It smelled like chamomile and honey. Perfect for calming her nerves. "I'm sorry to interrupt your morning."

"Oh nonsense. When you're as old as I am, this is right around lunchtime. Besides, Darla warned us you might drop by." The woman watched her over the rim of her mug with eyes that were both kind and discerning.

A large man walked in, absentmindedly pushing his arm into a well-worn blazer. His short, curly hair was beginning to gray. "Mama, why didn't you tell me we had company?"

"I'm not your secretary."

"Then I'm not your handyman," he said, bending down to kiss the old woman on her cheek. He stood and held out a hand. "Emma Day, I presume?"

"You presume correctly." She shook his hand.

"I'm on my way to the office. Let's chat on the way." He grabbed a worn leather folio and opened the front door, gesturing for Emma to follow. "Darla said I should answer whatever questions you have about the murder."

"I'm sorry to bother you at your home. I assumed the address Darla gave me *was* your office."

"Darla's nobody's fool. She wanted to keep it quiet that we'd talked. People love to gossip. Now what do you want to know?"

Emma felt a flash of panic when she realized she hadn't really thought about it. She would have to wing it. "Could you tell me from your perspective what happened yesterday?"

"Of course. When I arrived at the scene of the crime, the victim was dead. The director of the play had covered him with a sheet. I pulled back the sheet long enough to confirm what people told me. There was a single stab wound in the upper right ribs."

"Did you recover the murder weapon?"

"The people from County don't like it if you touch things. I took a hard look though. Big dagger, covered in blood."

"Do you remember if the murder weapon resembled the other prop knives used in the play?"

"It didn't just resemble the props. It *was* a prop knife."

"But... the prop knives are dull, and their blades push into the handle. They're harmless."

"Not if someone sharpened the blade and welded it in place. Wasn't the cleanest welding job—obvious if you were looking."

"But not necessarily obvious to someone whose attention was elsewhere."

"Exactly."

"Clarence told me that his knife was switched out for another. It seemed like just a convenient lie, but now you're making me think it might be possible."

"Definitely. Clarence was shaken up. He seemed as surprised by the stabbing as anybody. Kept saying, 'I killed him' to himself over and over."

"That almost sounds like a confession."

"No. He wasn't really talking to me. More like he was talking to himself, trying to get his head around what happened."

"Is that the sort of thing an innocent person does though?"

Marcus shrugged and was quiet for a moment before speaking. "I don't see a lot of murders, but I have worked with people in tough situations for most of my life. People never act how others expect them to." He thought for a moment.

"What do you mean?"

"Imagine you have a guy whose wife just died of cancer. How does he act?"

"I don't know. Sad?"

"You'd think. Or does he act relieved because she's not in pain anymore? Maybe he seems surprised—she fought so long he never thought it'd actually happen? Maybe he acts tough, trying to be strong for the kids."

"Point taken."

"People looking in from the outside expect a movie. They want people to act like something they'd see on TV. Folks don't work like that. So you can't just look at how the chairman behaved after and say it proves he meant to stab Harold."

They walked quietly for a while as Emma pondered what Marcus had told her. Then he surprised her by announcing, "We're here."

They had stopped in front of an office not far away from the community center.

"One last question: Do you know anyone who would want Harold dead?"

"I was wondering when you'd ask. If I had to guess, I'd say that it was tied up with the Reinhold account."

"Never heard of it."

"Lots of people are hoping you never will, I'm sure. Clarence and Harold were both partners at the same accounting firm. People are starting to whisper that they were helping Reinhold cook their books."

"Interesting… How would you know about that?"

"It's my job to get people to talk to me. Sometimes they talk too much," he said, unlocking the office door. He turned to Emma. "Don't hesitate to reach out if I can help. I like Clarence. Don't really want to believe he did it."

"I will."

"And Emma, be careful. If Clarence is innocent, that means there's a murderer walking around out there. No sense attracting their attention."

As she watched the door close behind him, Emma decided that she liked Marcus Walker. He had certainly given her a lot to think about. She'd have to look up Reinhold Industries when she got home.

But first, she needed to track down Clarence's wife, Clarice, though she didn't know where to find her.

CHAPTER 17
DEMONBUSTER

Emma was so wrapped up in her own thoughts that she almost ran into someone. It was an older woman in a pantsuit, carrying a portfolio. It took her a moment to make the connection.

"Gladys!"

Gladys looked her up and down. "You'd better learn to watch where you're going."

"I'm glad to see that you're able to walk a little better today. How's the ankle?"

"Awful."

"That's the spirit." Emma smiled at the old woman's comically gruff demeanor. "So... I talked with Clarence. He called me and asked for my help."

"Why on earth would he do that?"

"Clarence says he was framed, and he wanted me to follow a few leads for him. I'm trying to track down his wife. Would you happen to know where they live?"

Gladys laughed to herself, shaking her head. "He always was a chickenshit. Did the crime but can't stand the time. Don't tell me you agreed to help him?"

"Darla doesn't think he did it."

"That woman is entitled to her own opinions. It doesn't make them worth two cents."

The mention of Darla jogged something in Emma's memory. "Hey, I'm curious. When you sprained your ankle, you had me take you to an apartment nearby. But Darla referred to you as her neighbor."

The woman sniffed. "I own several properties. I come from a family of landholders. Now if you'll excuse me, we have an important vote coming up, and somebody's got to run the meeting."

"Sure, but first, could you point me toward Clarice's house?"

"It's on Westhill. Walk along Main until you get to the hardware store, turn right, and look up. But if it's Clarice you're after, you won't find her there."

"Why not?"

"Because she's right behind you."

Emma spun around and saw a woman in a hoodie exiting a building one block over. She was carrying a white cardboard box. Wherever she was going, she was going fast. Emma followed her.

As she passed the door the woman had exited, Emma saw a note pinned to it:

"Sanderson Accounting will be closed through the end of the week."

Emma felt an electric thrill. *So this is Clarence's accounting firm! But why would his wife be here? What's in that box?*

It wasn't hard to follow Clarice on Main's busy sidewalk, but when the woman turned in to an alley, Emma paused. She ducked out of sight and craned her neck to watch her.

The woman in the hoodie was quite a different figure from the perfectly coiffed lady Emma had seen kiss Clarence good luck. She seemed completely focused on her destination, not stopping once to check behind her despite being a woman in an alley alone.

Emma decided to risk it and followed. They passed silently together down the alley, through a gate, and into the core's expansive green. Clarice walked up the steps and knocked on the door of one of the many vacant houses.

When the door opened, Emma's blood ran cold. The person who answered the door was the man in the brown suit.

She found a bench and sat. Her brain was buzzing with questions. *Why was that man in that house? Was he a demon or a corporate shill? What was Clarice doing there? What was in the box?*

It was too much information. Too many questions, too many unknowns. It was like trying to solve a puzzle with way too many pieces. She needed to find a way to simplify the problem.

That was when she saw the robot.

———

On the other side of the green, a robot with a large antenna on its back waddled toward her. Emma squinted. *No, not a robot. It was Riley.*

They looked like a cross between a mechanic and a mad scientist: dark blue jumpsuit, hard hat, large backpack with protruding antenna. Straps ran across their shoulders and down to a tray, which held a laptop computer and a squawking walkie-talkie.

"Riley, you look like you're trying out for the Ghostbusters!" Emma laughed.

"Change that to Demonbusters and you'd be on to something." Riley stared at the computer screen. "We had a possible hit over by the library, but it didn't pan out."

"I saw the man in the brown suit just now, in that house." She pointed. "He was meeting with Clarice."

"Excellent. We've gridded off the core and will make it over there in a moment." Riley suddenly looked up from the screen. "If it's meeting with her, that could mean that she's the summoner!" They picked up the walkie-talkie. "Astrid, Mallory, we've got a live one. Meet me in sector 12B." Riley put down the walkie-talkie and began walking away.

"Where are you going? Aren't you going to go... bust the demon or something?"

"Bust the... Oh, you weren't joking. We study things. We don't... bust them. If the three of us triangulate, we can determine with a high degree of certainty if a demonic energy source is in the house."

"So what are you planning to do when you find the demonic energy source?"

"I don't know... follow it around? See what it does?"

"Science then."

"Yeah," Riley said, scanning the distance until two other figures appeared. "Looks like my crew is here. We'll take over surveillance of the house."

"Meow."

Emma felt a weight land on the bench beside her. Then she felt warm fur under her hand. "Oh hey, Captain. You're being nice this afternoon." She watched Riley walk away and join the others.

"Rrrrowl."

"What's the matter? Oh, that was my stomach, wasn't it? Let's go make lunch."

CHAPTER 18
LEATHERY WINGS

Back in her kitchen, Emma spread the last of her mascarpone on another toasted bagel. This one was sesame seed, and she overlaid the cheese with five translucent slices of Parma ham, a slice of tomato, and a spicy pickle from the farmer's market. She eyed her work, then cut the sandwich in half. The captain rubbed against her leg.

"Don't worry. I didn't forget about you." She gave him a little ham as a treat, then walked to the pantry and found a can of cat food, which she emptied into a bowl.

The captain walked over, sniffed it, and turned up his nose.

"What's the matter? It's tuna chicken medley—your favorite." She walked back to her sandwich. The cat tailed her. "Did I spoil you by giving you human food?" She gave him a little more ham, which he gobbled up.

She plated the sandwich and took it to the table, mouth watering in anticipation of the salty, creamy, spicy flavors. The pickle and tomato added a nice crunch, and the bread was toasted perfectly. The captain begged.

"Hey, your cat food's getting cold."

She took another bite, and the captain jumped onto the

table, making the whole thing shake under his weight as he landed. He walked around the plate, sniffing it, and then climbed into her lap, facing the table.

"I really don't think it's healthy for you to have so much ham. Is something the matter? You've never acted like this before."

From out in the hall came the sound of the cat door yawning open and then flapping quickly closed.

She froze, heart racing. If the captain was in her lap, what just came through the door? She looked down at the captain, who was absentmindedly licking his paw. "Aren't you supposed to spring into action now or something?" The captain didn't bother to respond.

That was when it happened. She was trying to figure out how to get the captain off her lap when another captain walked through the kitchen door.

Emma looked from one cat to the other. They were identical in every way: the black-and-brown fur, the green-and-yellow eyes, the snaggletooth. Her sandwich slid from her hand and plopped on the floor, giving the cat in her lap the chance he had been waiting for. He hopped down, extracted a slice of ham, and ate it.

It swallowed, then opened its mouth as if to yawn, but two large white fangs popped out. As it stretched, two leathery wings unfurled from its back. The thing pretending to be the captain tested them, then made a little hop and took to the air, wings beating lazily. It made a circle around the room then grabbed the light fixture with its claws and hung upside down.

Emma and the captain—the real one—were stunned into silence. Then the creature spoke to them. "What's the matter? Cat got your tongue?"

Emma looked up at the nightmarish creature, wishing she could crawl back into her warm bed to start the day over. She wasn't up for this kind of weirdness.

The captain was all about the weirdness—sinking his claws into it and biting it. He jumped from the floor onto the counter, then made a flying leap toward the creature, but he came up short. He was a fighter, not a gymnast.

The amused creature observed, "If you'll kindly instruct this uncivilized creature to calm itself, I would be happy to descend and chat."

"I think he's worried you're going to kill me or something."

The creature sighed. "That's what people usually think."

While they spoke, the captain had leaped up onto the breakfast table. From there, he did a running parkour jump, clearly having planned to land on the wall where he could sink his claws into the wooden doorframe to climb up. But the paint was too hard for his claws. He slid down with the sound of nails on a chalkboard.

"So you're not here to do any harm to me?" Emma asked, surprised by her own nonchalance.

"Of course not. What would be the fun in that? You're much more amusing alive."

"You're not really helping your case."

"Pardon me. It's been a few hundred years since I've spoken with your kind. There are bound to be a few cultural mix-ups. I only meant that if I killed you, I would only get to do that once. But if I refrain from killing you, a wide assortment of possibilities becomes possible."

Emma laughed despite herself. "You want to come down? Be my guest. But don't try any funny business, or the captain here will have something to say about it." She gestured to the captain, who was watching the creature warily.

"Thank you," it said, pushing off the ceiling. The demon did a flying somersault and landed in the chair next to Emma with a puff of smoke. When the smoke cleared, she saw that the creature had taken the shape of a man.

The "man" had an aristocratic bearing, was dressed in a

tuxedo with tails, and looked entirely comfortable in both the tux and human skin. A blue-and-white china tea service had materialized in front of him. He delicately poured a cup as the scent of jasmine filled the room and offered it to Emma. When she refused, he sipped and let out a sigh.

"Much better." The demon's voice was resonant, like a handmade cello. "The feline form has its delights, but it does rather cramp one. Now." He turned to Emma. "If you would like a moment to scream, rend your chest, flee in terror…"

"Why would I do that?" Emma picked up her sandwich from the floor, considered it for a moment, and then took a bite.

"It's not a necessity. I'd just assumed it was a customary human greeting. It's what people normally do when I introduce myself."

"I'm good. I'm used to losing my mind by now. Did you know that the captain over there is a novelist? He has his own typewriter."

"Do tell. I'd assumed he was merely the brute he appeared to be. My apologies." He gave a little seated bow to the captain, whose expression did not change.

"So what do you want? Why are you here?"

"Those are two very different questions with very different answers." He took a sip of his tea.

"I'm getting used to that too."

"What?"

"The vague answers. If there's anything the undead like, it's being mysterious. But I've had enough mystery today, so why don't you tell me plainly and save us both the hassle? You're the Waterloo demon, aren't you?"

The creature spit its tea. "Excuse me? The… Waterloo demon? While it's true, I've visited the Netherlands—"

"You're the demon that swapped the maps and made Napoleon lose the battle of Waterloo."

"Oh, trust me, he didn't need my help."

"But you were there."

"I can't believe this. I just—" He exhaled sharply. "I have existed for millions of years. I have been revered by no less than six civilizations as a god. And now, after being away for only a handful of centuries, I'm only remembered for a brief pit stop I made on the way to Brussels."

"We all stop being cool at some point."

"Imagine if you were to arrive to a party to find that everyone there was calling you a post office monkey. Just because you stopped at the post office on the day a certain diminutive narcissist got his comeuppance."

"I guess some things never change. But you never answered my question. Did you come to kill Harold Loftus?"

"The man at the play? Why, that's just what I wanted to speak with you about."

"You did kill him?"

"Heavens, no. Why would I do that?"

"Why else would you impersonate the captain, then turn into a bat and fly up to my ceiling?"

"I needed to talk with you about something of the utmost importance—"

"Did you put glitter in the first aid kit?" Emma interrupted.

"What? Oh yes. Delightful substance, isn't it? It flies absolutely everywhere. Impossible to clean. My sister hates it of course."

"Did the scripts go missing because of you?"

"Of course. How could I not take them? But to my credit, I did give them back. That's why I needed to talk—"

"It's your signature move, isn't it? Mixing things up?"

"I suppose you might say that, though I would argue that 'mixing things up' is a rather prosaic way to describe the disheveled, disordered glory that is me."

"So it *was* you who replaced Clarence's harmless prop knife with a working knife. You might not have stabbed him, but you killed him just the same." Emma scowled and looked away in disgust.

The demon sighed and rolled his eyes. "I *told* you that wasn't me, though I did appreciate the craftsmanship. The whole production was amazing, really." The demon smiled, remembering. "The most amazing thing I've experienced in my long existence."

"Can you prove that it wasn't you?"

"Why do you keep harping on this? Does it matter? It was a job well done. If the artist wishes to remain anonymous—"

"The artist? Someone was murdered. We take that seriously here in the real world."

"Do you? Well, in that case, it's simple enough to prove my innocence. Would you like me to do so?"

"I'm all ears."

"I sow disorder, or as you put it, mix things up. For me to do so, those 'things' must exist corporeally. The knife that you spoke of—from where did it come? I am certainly not capable of producing it."

"You produced that teapot."

"Yes, and when I leave, it will vanish. The knife, I imagine, has not disappeared in a puff of smoke."

Emma thought about that. "No, it hasn't."

"Well then, now that that matter has been dispatched, could we—?"

The demon was interrupted by someone pounding on the front door.

CHAPTER 19
AUDITION

Emma unlocked the door and opened it. "Hi, Riley, Astrid, Mallory— Hey, watch it!" she said, as the three researchers pushed past her into her front hallway.

Riley looked up from a device, which was beeping quickly. "Emma, find a closet and lock yourself in. You're not safe here."

"What are you—?"

"We've got a lock. It's just what you predicted," Astrid said, reading from a device.

Riley eyed the hallway wildly, then stormed into the living room where they proceeded to pick up and squeeze each pillow on the sofa.

"What are you doing, exactly?" Emma asked.

"Demons are shape-shifters."

"And you think a demon might have shape-shifted into a throw pillow?"

"They can be *anything!* You don't understand, Emma. We set up a perimeter around that house, scanned it up and down, but nothing was there."

"Could they have gone out the back?"

"That's just what we thought. That's how we picked up on the demonic energy signature that led us here—the Waterloo demon is *in the house*."

Mallory was back in the hall, pointing a box with a Y-shaped antenna toward the kitchen. "We're off the charts out here."

"Really? Have we done it? Have we really cornered the Waterloo demon?"

"Actually," Emma said, "he doesn't like to be called that."

———

The three applied folklorists stood around Emma's kitchen table, staring open-mouthed at the demon, who was pouring himself another cup of tea.

"Are they always so rude?" he asked Emma.

"I think they're more like the dog who caught the car. They're not sure what to do."

"May I offer a suggestion?"

"Sure," Emma said.

"Based on my interactions with humanity thus far, I believe the appropriate reaction would be panic."

"But you said you didn't come to hurt us." Emma said. Riley's crew seemed to relax a little at this revelation. Then they sprang to action, pulling out cameras, audio recorders, and notebooks. "So why are you here?"

"I'm here because I was summoned. Don't you know how any of this works?"

Emma decided to keep him talking. "Let's pretend I don't. Who summoned you?"

"Older fellow? Twiggy? Black cowl? I don't know. After the first hundred summonings, they start to blur together. The process itself is quite disorienting. One moment, you're frolicking in the nether regions—"

"Excuse me—what?"

"The nether regions. Home sweet home. The land of demons."

Emma laughed. "I think we might be getting lost in translation. You mean netherworld?"

He paused, thinking. "Nether*world*? No, that can't be right. It's not exactly large enough to be a world. I think it's more accurate to describe it as a region."

"It's just that the other word has a certain connotation— You know what? Never mind. You were telling us about being summoned."

"It's the usual story. I'm minding my own business, and then one day, I see a bright flash of light, and I'm trapped inside a circle in someone's basement. I'm assaulted by unpleasant odors and sounds while someone stands in the shadows and prattles on about slaying enemies, burning cities to the ground—that sort of thing."

"They wanted you to burn Undertown to the ground?"

"Perhaps? As I mentioned previously, they blur together. I usually have an intolerable headache at that point, so I rarely pay attention."

"This may sound like a silly question, but if you don't pay attention, how are you be able to do what they want you to do?"

"Do you mean to tell me that humans believe I have to do what they tell me?" He snorted a laugh. "That explains so much. You really are ridiculous creatures."

"So what are you doing here?"

"I was trying to explain that! For millions of years, I've roamed the nether regions—your world as well. My only purpose was to amuse myself. It was a dissipated existence. Then I saw the play..." His eyes lit up, as if remembering it. "The majesty of those words. The hushed whispers of the audience. The lights. The unearthly fog rolling off the stage. All ending in a final, climactic, ritual sacrifice."

Emma coughed. "Actually, the murder isn't usually part of it."

"Really?" the demon furrowed its brow.

"It's frowned upon."

"A shame, but I suppose I can live with a murder-less play." He laughed to himself. "Otherwise, the supply of actors would no doubt run short."

"There is that," Riley chimed in.

"In any case. I am here. I have seen my calling and am prepared to accept it. From now on, I will devote my existence to *the theater*!"

Riley was frowning, tapping their temple with an index finger. "So you want to be in the play? I'm not sure how I would cast a demon. And we don't typically just let anyone on stage. You have to do an audition."

"What's an audition?"

"It's where you prove to us that you're a good fit for the role."

"Well, that should be no problem at all! You've already seen my feline form." With a flash, the man turned into a snow-white cat. "Or perhaps you prefer something more dramatic!" The cat grew longer. Its face elongated, and its fur turned into the red scaly armor of a dragon. "No, no, you humans are so humanistic. You'd much prefer one of your own kind." There was another flash, and the demon turned into a perfect copy of Emma. "Hello, I'm just a clumsy girl with mommy issues."

"Watch it, buddy," Emma warned him.

"Not a method-acting fan? Then we can stick to the classics." He changed into the spitting image of Harold Loftus, dressed as Caesar, toga and all. "Et tu, Brute?" Then in a flash, he was back his original tuxedoed form. "Well, do I have the part?"

Riley laughed. "You would… if we had a play. We just don't know yet if the community will support a troupe where one of the actors murdered another. Even if we staged another performance, I'm not sure anyone would come."

Emma leaned toward the demon. "People usually avoid events that have a history of murder. Well, normal people, at least."

"You humans are nothing if not surprising. I would have thought the murder would sell more tickets. Still, you are the local experts," he said, eyeing them warily.

Riley thought silently for a moment, then spoke. "What if we could prove that it was a setup? Emma—"

"I don't have any proof. Just a lot of confusing leads that don't fit together."

"But you *do* have leads."

Emma turned to the demon. "You wouldn't happen to have taken the form of a man in a brown suit?" He shook his head. "Well, then I guess my main lead just evaporated. Still, there is the wife, Clarice. I could find out what she's up to."

"Great," Riley said, "and while you're doing that, we can start rehearsals up again."

"I can't promise anything. I might never find out who the killer is. I might find out that Clarence did it after all." Emma paused to think, then turned to Riley. "I'm going to need your help."

"Figuring out who summoned our new friend. I'm on it. We'll do a survey of the literature."

"We need to know not only how he was summoned, but *why*. Someone summoned a chaos demon into Undertown. They did it for a reason. Even if our friend wasn't involved in Harold's murder, perhaps the summoner was."

The demon raised a forefinger. "I would like to help with that if you do not mind. I rather like the idea of turning the tables on the person who summoned me from the nether regions."

"Excellent. You four work together on the paranormal

angle. I'll try to find out the dirt on Clarice— Oh, and I need to go online and look up Reinhold Industries."

"You mean *the* Reinhold Industries?" Riley asked.

"You tell me. There's a rumor that Clarence and Harold's accounting firm was cooking their books."

Riley let out a low whistle. "I can't believe you haven't heard about them. Their CEO is the richest man in America. He has kind of a cult following. I mean, the U-Dub business school is called *The Reinhold School of Business* for crying out loud."

"Some money's at stake then."

"Reinhold could literally buy some small countries if they wanted to."

"A lot of money then. Plenty of motivation for a murder." Emma grabbed a notebook from her purse and wrote down the important points of their discussion. She paused, turning to the demon. "I'm sorry, I never asked your name. What should I call you?"

"My name? It's unpronounceable. But for now you may call me Al."

CHAPTER 20
PINK SLIP

Emma couldn't figure out if the path up to Clarence's house was steeper than the path to Darla's or if her legs were just worn out. Sure, the idea of a hidden neighborhood surrounded by verdant hills and beautiful houses sounded charming, but try telling her feet that.

The house loomed before her, a dark shadow against the gray mist. A light shone from an upstairs window. Emma climbed the front steps and knocked on the door. When nothing happened, she knocked again and called out. No answer. She tried the knob, and it turned easily in her hand, the door creaking open a few inches. She peeked inside.

"Anyone home?" She strained to hear a reply, but it never came. "Clarice?" She pushed inside.

The hall was dark, except for a dim, flickering light in the room at the end of the hall.

Emma padded across the floorboards. "Hello?" She stepped into a large living room. A fire blazed in a stone fireplace, casting dancing shadows over the walls and ceiling of the elegant room.

To her right was a long dining table strewn with clothes

and toiletries. A large suitcase lay open on the floor. The room was otherwise empty.

What exactly is the plan here? She'd come to talk with Clarice, to size her up. But the way the door just opened… It threw her for a loop. Now she was here in the woman's living room—a woman who appeared to be about to leave in a hurry. What if she *was* the killer?

She began opening doors and peeking into the various rooms. First was a bathroom, perfectly clean, with soap shaped like seashells. Then a guest bedroom. Spotless. Bed tightly made with crisp sheets and fluffy duvet. An office…

Emma entered the office and flipped on the lights. It stood to reason that two high-powered accountants would have a home office. The two of them seemed to share it. There were two of everything. Two desks with oversized computer monitors. Two expensive ergonomic chairs. Everything was perfect… except the bookcase, which had been tipped over and lay on top of a pile of books.

She walked over and picked up a book. "*A Sawyer's History of Undertown.*" Another was titled: "*Pacific Northwest Frontiers: The Home Collective.*" She opened it and saw an inscription: "I hope you enjoy this as much as I did. – D. Reinhold."

Emma shook her head. *Did a local history buff ransack the place or something?* She put down the book and retreated from the office.

Upstairs, she found what she guessed was the bedroom of an adult child. It was still half-full of school mementos, photos, and stuffies but looked as though it was increasingly being used as overflow storage for the rest of the house.

Emma felt a pang as she looked at the photos of the young man with his friends. They looked so carefree and happy. A photo of the whole family caught her eye. It was propped on top of a stack of books on the bedside table. The whole family smiled happily at the camera, except for Clarice, who was looking off camera and seemed distracted.

Emma left the room, feeling a pang of jealousy over these people with their seemingly perfect family. She had to remind herself that things were not perfect anymore.

There was only one room left to search: the room with the light on that she'd seen from outside. She peeked in. It was chaos. Dresser drawers hung open and were half-emptied onto the floor. At the far end of the room, a window stood open, rain-soaked curtains blowing in the wind.

The floor was covered in fluffy white carpet, which was immaculately clean except for a patch by the window that was smeared with dirt. Looking more closely, she saw that it also contained pine needles and other debris from outside. Next to the stained patch of carpet were scattered several necklaces and earrings.

She looked around for any other clues as to what had happened there, but she found nothing. She stood and turned to leave when something moved.

There, in the mirror. It was a pale woman in a yellowing, frayed wedding dress. A lace veil obscured her face. She was looking out the window.

Emma froze, staring at the apparition in the mirror. *What exactly are you supposed to say to a spirit guide?* "Miss Havisham? Nice to meet you. I'm Emma." *Great job. What are you going to do, shake its hand?*

The spirit guide gave no indication of having heard her. She remained looking at the open window, placing a translucent sparking hand on the frame and leaning out.

Okay, she could just think it's weird that I'm talking to her reflection in the mirror.

Emma spun around, intending to approach, but in the moment that her eyes were off the apparition, she vanished, leaving behind only a misty silver scintillation where she had touched the window frame.

"Very mysterious. Good work," Emma said, annoyed. "Now let's see what you were looking at— Oh."

From the second floor, she couldn't make out the features of the unmoving body on the ground below. But it wore a baggy brown suit with a short red tie. A few feet away, a brown felt hat lay sopping in the mud.

————

"I didn't think I'd see you again so soon," said Marcus Walker.

"It's not a good look. I know." The cold had seeped into Emma's rain jacket. Underneath it, her clothes felt damp and clammy against her skin, and she shivered. Goose bumps prickled up and down her arms. "I came to talk with Clarice but found this guy instead."

She looked on as professionals photographed and measured the scene of the crime. Marcus nodded to her and led her to his car. He turned it on and let the heater run. "I take it you didn't know him personally?"

"I ran into him once in the core. He had a list and was trying to track down the owners of various properties. Then I saw him again today, meeting with Clarence's wife in a vacant house."

"You see an awful lot."

"I… was following Clarence's wife. I happened to see her leave his accounting firm with a box of documents. I… might have followed her."

"So you think she was the one who did in Harold?"

"I don't know. I'd heard rumors that she and Clarence were going through a rocky period. Then when I happened to see her, I just followed her without thinking."

"You need to get smarter, Emma. It's one thing to ask a few discreet questions. It's another to look through people's houses—especially people who might be dangerous. If you really think that she killed Harold, then what's to stop her from coming after you?"

Emma glanced toward the body and shivered. "I've learned my lesson. So what do they think happened here? How do you throw someone out a window?"

"She could have lured him in and gotten him to lean out the window. Then it would just be the matter of a well-placed kick and gravity would do the rest."

"I never really thought about the physics of it." She laughed to herself, then became serious. "You're right. I don't know what I'm doing."

"You're not the only one. If we keep having murders around here, we're going to have to get an actual detective one day." He sighed. "Hope it never comes to that."

Emma sat in silence, watching the technicians at work on the body. The window was still open above them. "Marcus, look up there. It looks like a piece of paper is stuck on the shutter." *Not just paper. Pink paper.*

"Where? Oh, good eye. Wonder what it says? I might be able to reach it from the window. Stay here." He got out of the car.

Emma waited a moment, then followed, wandering toward the house through the mist. She stared up at the piece of paper stuck under the shutter. It fluttered in the breeze for a moment before it became unstuck, tumbling down the front of the house.

Nobody else had seen it, so she picked the paper up and examined it. It was a list of addresses—the same kind of list the man had carried when they'd spoken in the core. Her eyes were drawn to the bottom-right edge of the page where it said PROPERTY OF REINHOLD INDUSTRIES.

CHAPTER 21
REINHOLD

Everything leads back to Reinhold, Emma thought as she took off her damp rain jacket and hung it on the coat stand. Then she absentmindedly stared out her front window onto the green.

Everything leads to them, but what do I know? Only that they're a big corporation with a dirty little secret that Clarence and Harold's firm was trying to hide.

She bit her lower lip and scowled. *The man in the brown suit was working for them. But why? Why do they care about some old vacant buildings in Undertown?*

Emma was startled out of her reverie by her phone buzzing against her hip. "You have a collect call from inmate 12947 at King County Correctional Facility. Press one to accept charges."

Really? She felt a flash of anger. Clarence was the one who'd gotten her into this mess to begin with. Everything she'd discovered pointed to his wife as the guilty party. Still, thinking of the man in prison, she felt a pang of pity stab her heart. She walked to her living room, sat down, took a deep breath, and accepted charges.

"So Emma, were you able to touch base with Darla?" Clarence said in his beige corporate monotone.

"I did. We spoke for a long time. She doesn't believe you're guilty. However—"

"Excellent work, Ms. Day. Now that you're on board with your *special abilities*, I expect that it's only a matter of time before my release. Now tell me, do you know who set me up?"

"You see, that's the thing—"

"If you were to ask me, my money would be on a powerful outsider. You know, the Neighborhood Association has been fighting for years to keep Undertown… Well, to keep it Undertown. I never thought they'd stoop so low."

"I'm sorry to tell you this, but the best lead I have is… your wife Clarice."

"My… wife?" He laughed. "No, you're mistaken. Or perhaps you're joking?"

"I've got an idea. Why don't you tell me about Reinhold Industries?" She swallowed hard, but her mouth was dry.

"Reinhold…"

"You recognize the name." Emma listened to the silence on the line.

"Of course I do. They were the firm's biggest client, contracting with us for their annual audits."

"Which you falsified."

"I did no such thing!"

"I heard you arguing with Harold Loftus right before the play. You offered him money. He refused."

"Yes, I did offer him money. I offered him the whole firm—"

"To keep him from talking?"

"No— Well, kind of, but—"

"I saw your wife leaving your office with a banker's box. She walked to the core and met with a man from Reinhold."

"You don't understand anything."

"A few hours later, I found the man dead outside her—I mean your house. Everything points at Reinhold, and Reinhold points back at you."

There was a long silence, and then Clarence finally spoke. "She wasn't acting on my behalf."

"Then why did I see her leave your office and meet with a man working for your client?"

Clarence sighed loudly, then said in a small, defeated voice. "It was her office too."

"Her office?"

"Clarice is a partner at the firm. She's actually my senior, having been hired two years prior. She was caught up in something bad, though I don't know exactly what it was."

"Are you saying that you weren't involved with Reinhold?"

"No. It was Harold's account." His voice sounded faraway and dreamy. "He brought them in, wined them and dined them. Turned on the charm—"

"Then why did you offer him money?"

"I was desperate, trying anything I could think of to get her out of that situation. But it was never just about money with Harold."

"You do realize that looks even worse for Clarice. If she wanted out of the mess she was in, and Harold was in her way—"

"She's not a murderer."

"It would have been so easy for her to replace your dull prop knife with a sharp one. She'd be rid of both you and Harold with a single stroke. I know your marriage was in trouble."

"That's ridiculous, not to mention impossible. I didn't have the prop knife with me at home. They were kept by the director and given out just before the performance. The prop master set out the knives and other props backstage just before the performance."

"Where exactly were they set out?"

"There's a door behind the stage that leads to a little hall. It's not a real backstage of course; it's not a real theater. But that hall is where we got ready."

"I'll have to verify that."

"Clarice isn't a murderer. But somebody out there is. With what she knows, I wouldn't be surprised if she's—"

Ding! "The conversation has been terminated." The robotic voice cut in.

Emma let out a huge sigh and threw herself sideways onto the couch. *Somewhere somebody is having a simple, normal day without any shocking revelations. What would it be like to be them?*

Her mind began to work. If they did set out the prop knives backstage, then finding who swapped the knife out could just be a matter of finding out who was backstage.

If the knife was welded open and sharpened, then the killer would need to have access to metalworking equipment, like a welder and grinder.

Who was backstage? Who has a welder? So much easier than demons and audits.

Her eyes fell onto the coffee table in front of her. On it were a stack of pages and a red pen. The captain's manuscript. She smiled to herself, sat up, and began to read.

Sassy looked at Colin. He knew him when he was just a kitten. He never would have guessed Colin would show up when he least expected it and save Sassy's life.

Colin sniffed the air keenly. "Cheeto, Snowball—all bought off by the Sandpiper. First, they only did it for the money, but once he got his hooks into them, they didn't have a choice."

"Rats, cats, people—they're all the same to him. Just tools to use and throw away." Sassy's voice was bitter.

"Come on." Colin beckoned with his head. "I know a place we can go. You'll be safe there, at least for the night."

Sassy hesitated for a moment before following Colin. He knew he could trust him. "I'm not sure there's a place in this city that's safe."

"There is," Colin said confidently. "I promise."

Sassy knew Colin could only be so confident because he was young. Sassy had been young once, but he followed Colin anyway because he had nobody else.

The tabby led him through a busy farmers' market. Overhead, humans went about their lives like they always did. Oblivious. The smells of the market pricked at Sassy's nose. Onions (fresh and rotten), earthy mushrooms, flowers that smelled like death.

They turned a corner. Colin pushed through a basement window and, from there, through a hole in the wall that led to a kind of tunnel.

"The old sewer system. It's been abandoned for years, but it's still safe. No one ever comes down here." Colin led him through the darkness, his paws leaving wet prints on the ground.

Sassy's heart sank. He had been reduced to hiding in the sewers like a rat. As they walked, one question stood out like a splinter in his mind: who was the Sandpiper?

Nobody knew. Nobody had ever really seen him except far in the distance, face hidden in a hooded robe.

Colin showed Sassy to a small room that had been cleared out. There was a mattress on the ground and a few blankets. It wasn't much, but it was better than nothing.

"This is where I stay," Colin said. "You can stay here too—for as long as you want."

Sassy hesitated for a moment. He was used to being alone. But he was tired, and he didn't want to be alone anymore. "Thank you," he said finally. "I would like that."

He curled up on the mattress and closed his eyes. Maybe

things would be different in the morning. Maybe he would wake up and this would all be a bad dream. But he knew that was just wishful thinking.

Emma finished marking up the pages, walked back to the captain's study, and put them on the desk. *The Sandpiper, huh?*

CHAPTER 22
COMPANION

"Emma, I've been looking for you!" a voice said behind her. She spun around.

"Will you *please* stop sneaking up on me like that, Dash? You just about made my spirit leave my body. Er… figuratively speaking."

"I was right. The captain *is* tracking something."

"Really? Did he meet up with the other members of the night watch?"

"No, I think he looked for them, but they were gone. Then he went out on his own. He would pick up a scent, follow it until it disappeared, then pick up the trail somewhere else."

"I think I know what he was hunting."

"Really?"

"I met a demon today. His name is Al. He wants to be an actor."

"Well, I suppose that would explain why the captain spent so much time near the old theater." He paused in contemplation, then spoke. "How can you be certain that it was a demon?"

"Lots of reasons. First, it took on the shape of the captain, jumped up into my lap, and rubbed its head against my palm." .

Dash was shocked. "The captain would never—"

"Second, when the *real* captain showed up, the demon cat sprouted a pair of bat wings and flew up to the ceiling."

"That does seem rather demon-ish, from a layman's perspective."

"Third—"

"There's a third?"

"The cat did a kind of somersault, there was a poof, and when he landed, he had transformed into an aristocratic guy in a tux."

"And he wants to be an actor?"

Emma simply shrugged by way of reply, then frowned, remembering her conversation with Clarence. "Hey, Dash, you were helping the play with atmospherics. Did you see where Riley laid out the props that the actors used?"

"Certainly. A small hallway runs behind the stage. The props were there."

"How were they arranged? Were they all in a big box?"

"No. Each actor was assigned a separate clear plastic tub containing their costume and props."

"Did they happen to be labeled?"

"Yes, by name. What's going on? Do you have a lead in Harold's murder?"

"It's hard to tell. Clarence claimed that someone swapped his knife out. I realized I need to understand how that could happen. Did you happen to see anyone unusual wandering around backstage?"

"Nobody in particular, but it wasn't unusual to find an assortment of people backstage. It is a hallway that services several offices, the janitor's closet, and the building's rear entrance."

"It sounds like anyone could have been able to sneak back there." She rolled her eyes. "Why can't things ever be easy?"

"Emma, I was wondering if you'd had a chance to search the library?"

"The library?" Her stomach dropped as she remembered the enormous mess of torn pages and how she'd promised Dash she'd figure out how to search it for information about his life. "No, I'm sorry. Things have been crazy around here."

"That's all right… I know you're busy."

"Hey, I gave you my word, and I'll keep it. It just may take a little while… but I know how we can get started!"

"How?"

"Before I can research your life, I need to know what I'm looking for." She walked into the kitchen, found a small pen and pad, and sat down at the table to take notes. "We've spent a lot of time talking, but I don't know many details about your life."

"But… there's so much I don't remember. Then when I start remembering too much, I disappear."

"I know, but you always come back, don't you?"

"So far, yes."

"And it's not painful or anything?"

"No, just a little disorienting— You're right. It's a risk I have to run if I'm going to learn about my past."

"Maybe we can start simply? Why don't you start with your birth and see how far you can get before you start feeling like you might disappear."

"Okay, I can give it a try, I guess. I was born in 1902 at Seattle General. My first memory as a child was lying in bed with a wet diaper, waiting on my nurse to change me. My initial education was provided by a private tutor and took place mostly in an unused office at the family firm."

"Perfect, you're doing great," she said, making notes and trying to keep up as he laid out the story of his early life.

His was the type of memoir that served the subject more than the reader. But Emma was happy to have the company. To listen to Dash's tale.

"...of course in those days, we called them Pep-O-Mints. I had just purchased some with my newspaper money when I ran into my good friend Davy. I didn't know at that time, but we would become devoted companions. At that time, we hardly—"

Emma glanced back at Dash and gasped. "Hey, Dash, are you okay? You're... flickering."

"It was only later when sculling—"

"Hey! Earth to Dash. Anyone in there?" she said, waving her hand in front of his face. The flickering was getting faster. "Maybe you should take a break."

"Of course I was much too tall to be coxswain."

Emma looked him in the face. "*Dashiell Gruber!* I would slap you if I could. Snap out of it!"

Dash disappeared entirely for three long seconds before popping back into existence. "What happened?"

"What do you think happened?"

"Oh... Did you record any useful information?"

Emma looked down at her sparse notes and tried to make herself feel more confident. "Definitely. Now I think you deserve a little rest. The couch is all yours."

Emma watched him float out of the kitchen, then turned back to her notes. *Davy, that could be a lead.* She tried not to think of how hard it would be to find anything in that library full of shredded books. She tried not to think of the countless people who had access to the backstage area where the prop knife had been switched for a real one.

You have to stay positive. Focus on what you can do. Emma was surprised to discover that there *was* something she could do. It was time to pay a visit to the scene of the crime.

CHAPTER 23
CONFETTI

The sidewalk around the community center was empty. Inside, most of the lights were off. She tried the door. Locked. What did she expect? Gladys could let her in— But wait... Hadn't Clarence said something about a back door?

Emma walked around to the back of the building. She walked past a dumpster and then around the side of the center where a low brick wall enclosed a tiny garden.

The gate swung open easily, and she walked in. Whoever had built this garden had really put their heart into it. Even in the fall, you could tell how lovely it must have been.

The door was right there, next to an overgrown rosebush. It was padlocked.

"Well, so much for that plan." She tugged the padlock in frustration, and it came undone. "Convenient..."

The door creaked as she pushed it open. Emma stepped through into a dark room that smelled of clay and turpentine. A little light filtered in from the open door behind her, but it wasn't enough to see by, so she felt around for a light switch and found one on the wall beside her.

When the light came on, she saw that she was in a utility

room. Coats, boots, and various garden tools hung from the wall. In one corner sat a potter's wheel. Next to the wheel was an old wooden door that led to a hallway.

Emma went in through the door. To her left were the offices that Dash had mentioned. The doors were nondescript, no nameplates. The tall, narrow windows above each door handle were covered with paper. One of them had, of all things, a photo of Mr. Bean taped to the glass, his eyes bulging.

In front of each door was a small wastepaper basket, apparently there for the custodian to clear out. Most of the bins were empty. One was not.

It was filled with long strands of pink paper, torn in the kind of ribbons one got from paper put through a shredder. Her heart sped up as she searched the bin.

Could it be? She dug through the pile, looking for something, anything, that could definitively link these shredded pages to the man in the brown suit. Perhaps even to the paper she'd found at the scene of the second murder.

What's that? She reached into the bin and pulled out a crumpled piece of the pink paper. The bottom of it was jagged and torn. *Looks like it jammed and they pulled it back out of the shredder.* Emma laid it on the floor and smoothed it out. There, at the bottom corner of the paper, were the words she was looking for: Reinhold Industries.

Gotcha.

Suddenly, the sound of a door slamming in the mudroom echoed through the hall. Emma scrambled to stash the corner of the page in her purse and looked wildly for somewhere to hide. It would *not* look good to get caught snooping. At the very least, Marcus would give her a stern talking-to.

There was a crinkling sound, then a *whoosh*—the sound of a garbage bag being opened.

She tried the door to the office in front of her. Locked, just like all the other offices.

She spun around and saw that on the opposite wall was a single door. No, not a door, a curtain. *The curtain that Dash talked about!*

As she pushed through, the dark, velvety material brushed her shoulders and fell heavily behind her.

Then she went blind.

CHAPTER 24
DUEL

"Ha, who comes here? I think it is the weakness of mine eyes that shapes this *monstrous* apparition."

No, not blind, Emma thought. It was a spotlight. She held her hand in front of her eyes and squinted.

"It comes upon me! Art thou any thing? Art thou some god, some angel, or some *devil*, that mak'st my blood cold and my hair to stare? Speak to me what thou art!"

As her eyes slowly adjusted, a shadowy figure strode impatiently in front of her.

"What is *she* doing here? I was promised the role of Caesar's ghost!" an aristocratic voice whined.

"House lights!" another voice said. At once, the room was filled with light, and the faint whine of fluorescent transformers filled the silence. "Emma? What are you doing here?" It was Riley.

"I'm not entirely sure." The room really was empty except for Riley, four other people, and the demon named Al, who looked very put out.

"Is this a challenge?" Al asked. "Is this another one of your human customs? Are we to battle, thespian versus thespian, for the ultimate prize: immortality in the limelight?"

Riley let out an exasperated sigh. "Al, that's not what's—"

"Well, I accept! Though I will warn you I am very hard to kill." He adopted a fencing pose, one arm held high above his head. A rapier materialized in his hand. He pointed it toward Emma. *"En garde!"*

"I'm not here to take your part, Al!" Emma said, dodging a thrust. "Will you cut it out!"

"Hey!" Mallory said, walking in from the shadows. "Demon boy! Eyes on me! Keep it up, and you won't get any part in the play. We'll make you hand out programs in the lobby."

The demon looked at her, hurt. "You people are no fun at all."

Riley turned to Emma. "It's been like this all day. You have no idea how hard it is to work with a literal chaos demon."

Emma thought back to some of her chemistry II lab students. She wasn't so sure.

Riley continued, "You're running a close second though. Why exactly did you burst onto the stage during my rehearsal?"

"Well, I was looking for something. I found it, but then I heard a noise, and I was worried that maybe a murderer had followed me here—"

"'Scuse me!" A ruddy face peeked through the curtain behind them. "Y'all have any trash bins that need emptied?"

"No, we're good. Thanks, Greg," Riley said. They turned to Emma. "So you were being chased?"

"Now that I have a moment to reflect, I do remember the sound of a trash bag opening. And the office trash cans were in the hall..." Emma sighed. "I was running away from the custodian, wasn't I?"

"Maybe you subconsciously want to be an actor?"

Emma looked around. "Um, no, thank you. I don't enjoy being perceived."

"Well, if Al doesn't get his act together, I might have to

draft you." Riley glanced at Mallory, who was busily taking notes. "Although we *are* getting some great research material out of this. It should be big enough to help Mallory make her big comeback, and it looks like Astrid might finally have a thesis project."

"Have you had any luck finding the person who summoned him?"

"Not yet. Apparently, being summoned can be quite disorienting, but little fragments come back to him occasionally. We're trying to piece them together and cross-reference them with the literature."

"I sincerely doubt someone sent him here to be in a play."

"No," Al interrupted. "It's always pettier than that. Kill so and so. Destroy such and such. Get me money. Get me power. It's just so easy to tune out. My sister is much better at that sort of thing."

"Killing?" Emma felt her stomach drop.

"No, remembering. But I shall make an attempt." He placed his fingers dramatically on his head and stared intently into space. "I'm getting something. A man. Purple robes. The crescent moon. A ship. That's… that's all." His shoulders and head slumped forward in a pantomime of exhaustion.

Emma looked at him. "It just doesn't make sense. Why summon a demon if he can't even remember what you want him to do?"

"Perhaps… for my personality."

"Definitely," Riley said in a monotone. "That has to be it. Now, as much as I'm enjoying this little conversation, it's over. Emma? Would you kindly get off my stage? We have a rehearsal to finish, and you have a murder to solve."

"Two murders, actually."

"Well, then you'd better get cracking."

CHAPTER 25
THERAPIST

Marcus Walker let out a low whistle as he leaned back in his easy chair and examined the pink paper that Emma had handed him.

Across from them, a log popped in the fireplace. Emma closed her eyes and savored the warmth that radiated from it.

Marcus looked up from the paper. "I have to admit, it is suggestive. I'm just not sure what it really suggests." He set the paper on a side table, then retrieved a bottle and poured a small amount of amber liquid into a waiting cup. He took a sip. "You say that you found it at the community center? You weren't getting into trouble, I hope."

Emma squirmed in her seat. The sofa's vinyl cover made it hard to get comfortable. "I was at the community center, watching the rehearsal, and happened to see it in a trash can." The fact that she only saw it after digging through the trash can for several minutes was a mere technicality.

"It's the same kind of paper we found at the second murder scene. It says Reinhold Industries at bottom. Seems reasonable to assume that this page came from the same document that was taken from the second victim." He took a sip from his glass and exhaled. "I wonder why you'd kill a man for something, then run it through a shredder."

"Maybe the killer wanted to stop the information from getting back to Reinhold."

"But does it make sense if Clarice is the killer? Didn't you see her and the victim working together? She could have stolen the papers if she wanted them so badly." He was silent for a moment, then spoke. "Did you happen to notice where you found this paper?"

"I told you—"

"No, I mean whose office did this come from?"

"The bins were all out in the hall." She strained to remember. "But the nearest office door had a picture taped to the glass. Monty Python? No, it was Mr. Bean, that English character from the nineties."

"That would be Clarence's office." He picked up his glass and drained it. The ice cubes clinked as he set it on the table. "I have to tell you this doesn't look very good for Clarice—or Clarence, for that matter."

Emma leaned forward, cupping her head in her hands. "You're right. I don't know why he would want me mixed up in all this. Most of the evidence I find points back to his wife."

"So you admit you're mixed up in all this." Marcus laughed. "You know, you don't have to be. There's enough trouble in this world. Why look for more?"

Emma thought back to her call with Clarence, feeling torn. "I talked with him earlier today. He called me from jail. He was totally convinced that Clarice was innocent, even though so much of the evidence points to her."

Marcus shook his head and regarded Emma with a dry smile. "That man is head over heels in love with his wife. He'd do anything for her."

"Really? I heard that they were on the rocks."

"Anybody who thinks love's not rocky from time to time has a big surprise coming."

"He said that she was in over her head with the Reinhold account. He also said that Harold oversaw that account."

"So they were working together?"

"Right before Harold was murdered, I saw him and Clarence arguing. Clarence was trying to pay him off, but Harold refused. He told me he was trying to get Harold to leave his wife alone."

"I'm intrigued," Marcus said, reaching around to the base of the side table. He grabbed a bottle and poured himself a refill. "There's not much that goes on in this town that I don't hear about, but this is all news to me."

As Marcus leaned back in the easy chair—rumpled, a little tired, but comfortable—it occurred to Emma that he would be around her dad's age. Too bad she'd never known her dad.

Emma shook herself, coming back to the present. "Maybe he loved his wife so much he killed Harold to protect her."

"Remember you only have Clarence's word that Harold was in charge of Reinhold. Maybe Harold was innocent, and Clarice killed him before he could expose her."

"Or maybe they're working together. I… I don't want to believe that Clarence could call me up and lie so easily to my face."

"It happens. People disappoint you. Doesn't always happen, but often enough."

"Did you used to be a cop or something?"

The man's face wrinkled with mirth. "Me? A cop? That's a good one. I'm the opposite of a cop."

"What? Are you saying you're a criminal?"

"Worse. I'm a therapist," he managed, laughing. "I wanted to help heal my community. That was the plan, at least. Nowadays I mostly check in on people. Make sure the old folks have food in their cupboards. Find help for people who can't make the rent."

"And you're the liaison with the county sheriff."

"That used to be Pope's job, but—"

Emma's face darkened at the mention of the man who killed her cousin.

Marcus noticed. "I'm sorry. It was inconsiderate of me to bring that up. It must have been difficult for you."

"It's okay." Emma shook her head and tried to smile. "I just forget sometimes that any of that happened. It's always a shock to remember."

"It was a shock to all of us. I hope I never get used to murder." He looked into the distance for a moment. "It's not only a shock, it also takes me away from my real work. We have a full-blown housing crisis. People can't afford to live here."

"Really?"

"House prices keep going up. Landlords see that and raise prices on their tenants. I'm working on a case now of an old woman who's rented the same apartment for twenty years, and they just doubled her rent."

"That's awful."

"It's the world we live in." They spent some time looking at the fire in silence. Then he turned to Emma. "That reminds me… I have some case files I need to look over before my mama gets home from bingo and makes me watch reruns with her."

"Say no more. What are you going to do with the paper?"

"The same thing I do with everything else: hand it over to the county. I just wish we had the rest of the pages."

CHAPTER 26
DATE

The streetlights were clicking on as Emma made her way to Main from Marcus's house. The afternoon mist was turning into a heavier drizzle. She zipped her jacket and pulled up the hood.

As she walked, scents rose up from the yards she passed and from the hills overlooking the neighborhood. The spice of fallen leaves mixed in with the fresh tang of pine sap. They blocked the noises of Seattle beyond, making Undertown feel like its own little world.

I just wish we had the rest of the pages. The words echoed in her mind. If the killer wanted the document destroyed, shouldn't she want it to be recovered? *But how?* It was a shredded, disorganized mess.

She shivered as a mass of cold air rolled through boughs of cedar and spruce, down the face of Westhill into Undertown. The world, by imperceptible degrees, grew whiter as the chill turned damp air into fog. She walked faster.

Warm light spilled from windows of the houses that she passed. She saw figures moving inside. They were families—normal people. They weren't cold and alone, trying to find a killer. Even Marcus had his mother and his fireplace.

A pang of sadness tore at her heart. Why couldn't she have a normal family, complete with the zoo trips and movie nights? Why did she get the crazy mother hell-bent on protecting her from supernatural terrors? Why did she keep finding dead people?

I just wish we had the rest of the pages. Hadn't the custodian thrown them out?

To her left, the window of the Tigress was dark except for two illuminated mannequins dressed in the latest fashions appropriate for "the woman of indeterminate age." The windows above the store were dark as well.

Ever since Emma had broken the curse that hung over the core, Diedre had been elusive. At first, Emma thought she'd been embarrassed about her part in creating the curse. However, when her absences lengthened, Emma began to think maybe it was something else. Though she would never admit it, she had started to miss the mysterious, fashionable older woman.

Viv might know what had happened to her. The two had a history.

Ahead, the windows of the Undertown Community Center were also dark. *The theater kids must have gone home.* She stopped and stared at the building. *Wouldn't the shredded document be in the dumpster just behind the community center?* As she stood and stared, the rain picked up and pelted loudly against the hood of her raincoat.

She turned away to walk toward the alley she knew would take her someplace warm.

———

The coffee shop was a welcome relief to Emma as she pushed through the heavy door. It was late now, and only a few patrons remained at Deadtown, nursing the last sips of their coffee.

Viv looked up from wiping the counter. She smiled when she saw Emma and tossed a bag of chamomile into a mug, filling it with hot water.

Emma waved as she slipped out of her soaked raincoat. The green velvet couch was empty. She walked over, draped her jacked over the back, then sat on the floor directly in front of the electric fireplace. The dry heat of the imitation fire seeped into her bones, relaxing her tight muscles. She leaned back against the couch and stared into the flickering flames of the electric logs.

"Heya, Em," Viv said, handing her the steaming mug of chamomile tea. Tea delivered, she sat beside Emma.

"You have no idea how much I needed this." Emma blew on the tea, then carefully took a sip. Warmth spread down to her stomach and then out to the rest of her body. "It's been a heck of a day. You know that guy in the brown suit we were looking for?"

"The one you thought might be some kind of demon? Riley might have mentioned it."

"Well, he's not a demon. He's dead. I found him outside Clarice's window."

"Dude, that's messed up. Are you okay?"

"I was going there to talk with her. Now she's nowhere to be found, and he's been thrown out the window."

"Wow. It's hard enough to throw somebody out a door."

Emma laughed. "Of course you'd know all about that."

Viv grinned and gave an exaggerated shrug. "Hey, it's not my fault it's rougher around here. Sometimes a guy needs to be ejected."

"Well, this guy got ejected, for sure. We found a piece of paper that showed he was working for a company that's been up to some shady stuff."

"Isn't that, like, all of them?"

"Well… yeah. But this particular company, Reinhold, is enormous, and supposedly they've been cooking the books.

The firm that does their audits is none other than Clarence and Harold's. Hey, I just remembered I snapped a picture. Wanna see?" Emma pulled up the photo and handed Viv her phone.

"Wild. It's a bunch of addresses?"

"He was looking for the owners."

Viv squinted at the photo, then zoomed in. "There are only twelve addresses here. There are way more than twelve buildings in the core."

"The rest of the pages are missing. Well... not missing. I know exactly where they are."

"Great!"

"The only problem is that they're shredded and all mixed up."

"Not so great." Viv frowned for a moment, then looked up. "Hey, I wouldn't be surprised if Riley knew some people who could unmix them."

"How could they do that?"

"Computers? AI? I'm not the smart one here. But look, Riley works at a huge university. I wouldn't be surprised if someone there could take a bunch of photos of some shredded paper and run them through some AI that would put the pages back together."

"That sounds... implausible. But it doesn't sound impossible. Can you come with me?"

"Me? Ummm..."

"Seriously, it's dark out there. It's raining. I'm not sure I'm up to going on a solo dumpster-diving expedition."

"Tonight?" Viv glanced at her watch. "But I'm just about to close up."

"Perfect, I can wait. It'll give the rain time to slow down and give me time to warm up."

"No, I mean I just have to be somewhere," she said, running a hand through her short hair.

"Really?" Emma grinned, amused at Viv's apparent nervousness. "What's up?"

"I just… have a date."

"What! With who? Diedre?"

"No— Ew. I mean, yeah, I went out with her like three times, but that was twenty years ago. It wasn't the best decision, but—"

"Sorry! I just had her on my mind. Her store's been closed for a while."

"Well, don't ask me. I mean, we're back on speaking terms, but that's it. She's probably gone off to the witches convention— What? I'm only half joking." Viv snorted, then smiled nervously. "You wouldn't know her. Anyway, we're going topside. Going to do dinner and a movie."

"Eeee! So exciting!"

"Well, don't reserve a U-Haul for me just yet. I've learned my lesson. I'm taking it slow this time."

"That's great. So you'll have time to watch my back at the community center? It'll just take five minutes."

Viv looked at Emma like she was an unsolved puzzle. "You know what? Why not?" She stood and addressed the room. "All right, everybody! Shop's closed for the night! Get out if you don't want to get kicked out!"

CHAPTER 27
TRASH PANDA

The rain began to let up as Emma and Viv left the coffee shop and walked to the community center.

"So you guys really found a demon? That's... not a question I ever thought I'd be asking."

"It kind of found us," Emma admitted.

"It's just... You spend all your life hearing spooky stories about demonic possession. Then to have one in the flesh—it does have... flesh?"

"I think a demon has whatever it wants to have. Right now this one looks like an aristocrat from 1897, and he wants to be an actor."

"I've known a few actors. It tracks." Viv peered into the darkened front window of the community center. "Looks empty enough." She tried the door. "It's... open. You would think they'd have better security after what happened."

"We're not going in. The dumpster is around the back." She rummaged through her purse and pulled out a large flashlight. "The bag should be pretty close to the top—"

"Hey, you kept it!"

"What?" Emma looked around in confusion.

"The flashlight."

"Oh yeah. I use it all the time." She flicked it on. "Anyway, we'll find the trash bag full of shredded pink paper, grab it, and be out of here before anyone's the wiser. Come on."

They went around the side of the building. In the dark of the night, the pea patch took on a witchy aspect. In the flashlight's moving beam, decomposing tomato and bean plants looked like fingers reaching up through the loam.

"It's over there," Emma said, spotlighting the dumpster. Its blue paint was flaked, revealing rusted, pitted steel underneath. The large plastic lid attached to its back was closed, hiding the contents. Emma reached and awkwardly pushed the flap up, letting it pivot and swing down, crashing behind the bin. She winced.

"Oof, might want to be a little quieter," whispered Viv.

Emma peered over the edge of the large metal container. Two shining eyes looked up at her and lunged.

Emma jerked backward, lost her balance, and fell into Viv who caught her. Her heart was pounding so hard she thought it would leave her chest. "What was that?"

"What? I didn't see anything."

"Something is in there! Some kind of animal." Emma blushed, realizing that she was being held up by Viv. "Sorry." She righted herself and trained her flashlight on the dumpster. From inside came a *boom*, then a scratching, scraping, scrambling noise.

Two paws found purchase on the lip of the dumpster, and a feral, black-and-white face emerged. Emma and Viv began to laugh as the enormous raccoon struggled to lift itself out. The raccoon reached its tipping point at the lip and fell, flailing, onto the ground. Once it righted itself, it glared at them.

"I guess raccoons don't land on their feet like cats," Viv said. "Hey, little buddy, you okay?" Viv said, stepping forward.

"What are you doing? Don't touch it!"

"He's just a little lost trash panda. I mean, look at him. He's a little chunk!" They watched as the raccoon lumbered to the cedar fence, tried to climb it, but slid back down. "Do you think I should give him a little boost?"

"No! Those things have rabies."

"Oh, calm down. I wasn't really gonna. Hey—good job, buddy!" she said as the raccoon scrambled to the top of the fence, balancing there for a moment before flopping off and falling to the other side. "How can you not love a little guy like that?"

With the animal safely away, Emma once again approached the dumpster. This time it contained only trash. She found a stick and poked around. "It's a clear plastic bag with a bunch of shredded pink paper."

Viv peered over the edge and pointed. "Hey, is that it?"

"Yeah! Can you reach it? You have longer arms than me."

Viv leaned over the edge, stretching out her arm, but she was nowhere close to reaching it. "That's a negatory."

"Okay, then hold my purse and give me a boost."

"You're… really going to get in there? I mean, little buddy was just having dinner. It's kind of messy in there."

"Unless you have another way that I can get the bag."

Viv pondered for a moment, then bent over, weaving her fingers together into a platform for Emma to step on. "I never pictured myself as a cheerleader."

"Go team." Emma stepped into Viv's hands and stifled a scream as she was thrown headlong into the dumpster, landing with a crunch.

The inside of the dumpster smelled like pizza and coffee grounds. She touched her hair, felt something slimy, and sniffed her hand. Correction: *she* smelled like pizza and coffee grounds. "I'm going to need to take the world's longest shower when I get home."

"You know, you probably shouldn't be so loud. We're technically not supposed to be here," Viv said in a low voice.

Emma rummaged around. Sounds of rustling trash bags and crunching aluminum cans spilled out of the dumpster. "I think I've got it!"

"Okay. Grab it, and let's get out of here."

"Hold on, it's stuck." Sounds of rustling bags and tinkling glass spilled out of the metal enclosure. "Okay, I've got it! I'll toss the bag out to you in three... Two... One."

The sound of ripping plastic accompanied a bursting plume of pink streamers that launched skyward, lost momentum, then tumbled back down into the dumpster—and onto Emma.

"That doesn't look good," Viv deadpanned.

A creature loosely resembling a pink porcupine looked over the edge. "Hand me my purse."

"What?" Viv looked at Emma, covered in damp, disintegrating strands of pink paper, and tried very hard to remember the seriousness of the situation. She failed, laughing. "You should see yourself! You look like a Muppet."

"Hand me my purse!" When Viv complied, she scraped a handful of the confetti off her face and plopped it in the bag.

"Don't you think we might chalk this one up to lessons learned and get out of here?" She looked at her watch.

"You can go, but I came to get this freaking document, and I'm going to get it."

"But it's... everywhere now. You'll be lucky to pick up half of it."

"I don't care," Emma spat, furiously scooping up strands of shredded paper. "Go. Have fun on your date. I'll do this by myself." She glanced up at Viv, who wore an uncomprehending expression. A long moment passed. "I'm sorry— Look, I think I've got it all." She held up her purse, which was bulging with shredded paper and stained with pizza sauce. "Help me down."

Viv spent a moment in thought. "Sure."

Emma handed her the purse, then boosted herself up to the dumpster's mouth and swung her legs over.

Then she went blind.

CHAPTER 28
BUSTED

Emma and Viv were lit up by a light positioned directly in front of them.

"Just what in Sam Hill is going on here?" a voice asked from behind the light.

Emma lost her balance and slid off the edge of the dumpster, crashing into the mud below. Here and there, strands of pink paper still clung to her.

"Now what the heck are you supposed to be? Emma? What are you doing here acting like some kind of pink... raccoon?" The light clicked off. After a moment, Emma saw that it was Gladys. She was holding an enormous flashlight. "I thought you had enough sense not to take up a life of crime."

"Life of crime?"

"Who else but a criminal would break into the community center? Don't try to deny it! Silent alarm. And you," she said, turning to Viv. "Vivian, what would your mother say?"

The large woman shrugged.

"We're not criminals," Emma finally said. "We're looking for evidence related to the murders."

"There's been another? Oh dear," Gladys said as she raised a hand to her mouth in a gesture of surprise. "But what would you be doing here? Harold's murder hardly needs to be investigated, does it? Or do you mean to tell me you *believe* that man?"

"I just want to find the truth, whatever it is."

Gladys squinted at them and shook her head. "It our own fault, really. I mean, the Neighborhood Association."

"Are you saying that the Neighborhood Association was responsible for Harold's death?"

The woman laughed. "No, child. It's our fault that whenever something like *murder* happens around here, amateurs like yourself feel the need to nose around 'the truth.'" She sniffed. "Undertown has clung to its independence for so long that we've fallen behind. In the very near future, this sort of thing will be handled by the Seattle Police Department."

"The SPD?"

"No more amateur sleuths nosing around in crimes, putting themselves in unnecessary danger, tampering with evidence."

"I thought that the county sheriff was in charge."

"Yes, but they're so remote, aren't they? As soon as the board passes the measure next week, we'll have our very own SPD precinct. And *I* won't have to get out of bed to deal with trespassers."

"This is the community center, isn't it?" Emma said, feeling anger rise in her chest. "I'm part of the community. How can I be trespassing? And I'm not 'nosing around.' I'm trying to make sure that an innocent man isn't locked up for a crime somebody else committed!"

"This is nonsense. Who would go to such crazy lengths to frame Clarence?"

"Does the name Reinhold ring a bell?"

Gladys's eyes narrowed. "Of course it rings a bell. You

think *she* did it?" She paused in contemplation, then grinned. "I suppose anything's possible."

"Hold on a second, what do you mean by she?"

"You don't know? She was a client of your aunt's. I would have thought Cora told you all about her."

Emma felt a stab of anger at her departed aunt, who hadn't taught her anything. "She didn't."

"Well, you're not going to get any more information out of me. I don't condone your snooping. Yours either, Vivian." Gladys began walking away, then turned. "Emma, I'll tell you this as a friend, even if you don't want to hear it. You don't want to get mixed up with the Reinholds. You don't grow the family business into one of the biggest companies in the world without learning to be ruthless."

As Gladys walked away, the rain began to pick up again. Emma turned to Viv, "I'm sorry for snapping at you. It's hard for me to let go sometimes."

"Hey, you're human. It's okay."

Emma grinned sheepishly. "Thanks, Vivian."

"Don't you dare call me that name," Viv said, blushing. "Can you believe I took piano lessons from that woman when I was a kid? I never saw a house with so many doilies."

"I guess you'd better go get ready for your date," Emma said, as they began walking back toward Main Street.

"Yeah. Remind me again, how do you talk with people?"

"Oh, shut up. You're going to do fine," Emma said, snapping her bulging purse shut.

"I'm not feeling great about your chances to ever get that paper back together. I know I said Riley could help, but I hadn't seen how mangled it was. And now it's all wet and mushed together."

"You're probably right, but I've come this far. Might as well take it home and dry it out," Emma sighed. As they rounded the corner toward Main, the rain made the pavement glisten with reflected light. "You know, Viv, I like sneaking around at night with you."

"Yeah… it's fun. It's making me feel like a kid again, especially since we got scolded by a grumpy old lady."

CHAPTER 29
SABOTAGE

Emma unlocked her front door, opened it, and switched on the light.

"It's just me," she announced to the empty house. She made her way to the kitchen and laid a towel on the counter next to her pile of *Scientific American* issues. Then she began to carefully spread out the damp wad of pink confetti to dry on it.

She yawned as she fixed herself a cup of chamomile tea, lifting the steaming mug to her nose and inhaling deeply. She wanted to sleep. She wanted to curl up into bed with a mystery and read until words blurred together on the page and the book began to fall from her hands. Then she'd reach over, turn out the lamp, and drift into pleasant dreams.

But she couldn't—not with so many unanswered questions.

She climbed the stairs to the second-floor bedroom she had converted into her office. Flipping on the light, she walked over to her desk and placed her tea on a ceramic coaster shaped like a penguin.

Next to the desk was an old rusty army-green filing cabinet. It looked like it had served in World War II and possibly even taken a couple of direct hits from enemy artillery. Fortunately, it somehow was still functional.

This was the filing cabinet she'd found in Aunt Coralee's attic. It contained the case files for all her aunt's cases—psychic detective cases.

If one of the Reinholds lived in town and had been a client of her aunt, then their case information should be in this filing cabinet.

She opened the drawer labeled A-L. The metal drawer slid open smoothly and caught with a *clunk*.

Her aunt's organization method had been straightforward. Inside the drawers were hanging file folders, one for each letter of the alphabet. Inside those hanging folders were the actual case files, neatly alphabetized.

She found the hanging folder labeled *R* and spread it open, thumbing through the inner folders.

Rael. Rabel. Reinhardt.

That was easy. Too easy, she realized as she pulled the Reinhold folder and realized that it was totally empty.

She stood there for a moment with a feeling of déjà vu. It had been only months ago that a missing folder had led her to finding Jessie's killer. Could it be happening again?

She pulled up a chair and sat down at her desk. She placed the folder on top of the desk.

Perhaps the folder itself contained some clue. She turned it over, hoping to find something, even a note written on the inside of the folder.

Nothing.

Emma remembered how Riley and their crew had set up a photography station on the top floor of Cora's house and photographed and tagged each page in the case files. They were, in Riley's words, "A holy grail of local folklore," since Coralee was at the center of so many things going on around town.

Maybe Riley's students had a mix-up, she thought. After she discovered the case files, she allowed Riley's research team to scan and catalog them. *They might have simply misplaced the papers when they put them back.*

She pulled open her desk drawer and rooted for the thumb drive that Riley had given her. It contained a searchable index of all of Aunt Cora's case files. She plugged it into her computer, opened the index spreadsheet, and searched for Reinhold.

Nothing. She scanned the list for any names that resembled "Reinhold," in case they'd simply misspelled it. Again, nothing.

At least she could go to bed now. She pushed her chair away from the desk, but before she could stand up, an instant message notification popped up on her screen.

It was from Riley. "Hey, we got a lead on the summoner. Our demon started remembering. Want to go on an expedition?"

Remembering, huh? "Was he able to tell you who summoned him?" Emma replied.

"Not exactly… He remembers the place. The full moon helped him. He remembered a big sculpture. Specifically, a large bas-relief sculpture of a crescent moon. It was right above the spot he was summoned."

Emma searched her memory and typed back, "I don't think I've seen anything like that."

"I have. Here. Take a look at this picture I took when we were looking at the theater for restoration."

Emma squinted at the image on her screen. At first, she didn't understand what she was looking at. The photo, having been taken with a flash in a dark room, was extremely bright in the center and dark around the edges. She stared at it for a moment, and then it made sense. It was an old plaster wall with faded, chipping paint. On it was depicted, in relief, a half-moon surrounded by dancing women in gauzy robes. "It's kind of art deco."

"It's just to the right of the stage at the old theater."

"I bet Al loved finding that out," Emma typed.

"Tell me about it. Now he won't shut up about how he was born in the theater. We're heading there now. Wanna come?"

Emma glanced at the clock. *Couldn't this wait until morning?* She longed to walk down the hall to her bedroom and collapse onto her mattress. But she knew she'd never be able to sleep knowing that Riley was chasing a demon summoner through an abandoned theater only a few blocks away.

"Sure. I'll be there," she finally replied. "But first... Do you know anything about my aunt's Reinhold file? All I have is an empty folder. There are no entries in the spreadsheet you gave me."

"Really? I could have sworn I scanned those documents myself. Let me check my database."

Emma took a sip of her tea as she waited, staring at the computer screen, and felt herself come back to life. The office needed a little work, and her mind began to wander as she pictured it. New blinds. A chair other than a cheap, spinny backbreaker. A little art on the wall. Once her office was perfect, it would be so much easier to write up those cover letters and prep CVs. You couldn't do serious work like that on a rickety old desk.

Emma saw movement on her computer screen as a new message appeared. She leaned forward and read.

"I checked our document management system, and there are no entries for Reinhold. It's troubling that they aren't here. I'll meet with the team tomorrow and see if there's anywhere else they could be."

An idea flashed into Emma's mind. "Could it be Al's fault?"

"Interesting hypothesis. Let me ask him." There was a pause. "No, he swears he had nothing to do with that."

"But he's literally a demon, isn't he? Could he be lying?" Emma replied.

"I'm not entirely sure it's ever occurred to him to lie. But speaking of the demon, I think we'd better head to the theater now, before he goes by himself."

Emma finished her tea and set the empty mug on the desk. She was going to pay for all these late nights out, but what choice was there?

"Coming," she typed. Then Emma closed the screen of her laptop and leaned back precariously far in her roll-y office chair. Why did she keep getting into situations like this?

Why did it matter?

She hauled herself up out of the chair and noticed the captain staring at her from the doorway, looking a little more rugged than usual. "What? I read your pages. Seems to be getting a little dark, but I'm into it," she told him.

The cat padded away.

"Fine," she said to the empty room, then stood and yawned. She put the empty Reinhold folder back into the file cabinet and headed downstairs. As she put on her raincoat, she stared out her front window onto the darkened green, where even the houses that had residents were turning their lights out and going to bed.

CHAPTER 30
PENTAGRAM

The theater was a short walk, but it was a dark one since the streetlights weren't working. When the core was cursed and abandoned, the Neighborhood Association had disavowed it. Now that the curse was gone and the first few new residents were trickling in, nobody knew whose job it was to fix things like the streetlights.

She reached the dark entrance of the theater, playing her flashlight across its darkened facade. The moving light cast shadows that almost seemed alive. Riley and crew were nowhere to be seen.

Tentatively, Emma reached out to the tall brass bar affixed to the door. It was damp and cold to the touch. She pulled, and the heavy wooden door swung open. A wave of musty air rolled over her, smelling of dust, fungus, and pigeon droppings.

Entering, Emma let the door close behind her, and she hugged herself for warmth. The building was cold in the way that only a building of brick and concrete, unheated for forty years, could be. It was quiet except for a far-off pounding sound.

"Riley?" she called, looking around the foyer. At one end

was a ticket counter. At the other end was a concession area with a machine that held a single desiccated hot dog. The old carpet was red, though thickly covered in dust, and damp footprints led away from the front door.

Easy enough. Follow the footprints.

They led past a wall of posters to a pair of elaborately carved double doors. The brass push plate was smooth under Emma's palm, and she pushed one of the doors open, walking into the auditorium.

Far ahead of her in the darkness, the pounding sound was accompanied by muffled voices. Pointing her flashlight at the stage, she saw only a heavy red velvet curtain. Dust swirled in the light.

It's like a tomb, Emma thought as she looked up at the low ceiling. Finally, she realized she was standing under what must be a balcony.

As she followed the footprints down the aisle, the ceiling receded into invisibility, far above her. The spaciousness was only enhanced by the darkness. Far above, a pigeon cooed and flapped its wings.

The sound of voices grew louder as she followed the footprints down the aisle to a set of stairs and up to center stage. Finally, she stood in front of the heavy red velvet curtain, dust tickling her nose. "Riley? Astrid? Hello?" She sneezed, and the sound echoed back to her from the empty room.

"I have the impression that the designer was more interested in visual ornamentation than in practical acoustic design." Al said as his face peered out from behind the curtain. "Still, it is a marvel!"

"A dusty marvel... that smells a little too much like pigeon," Emma retorted.

"I thought it provided a nice ambiance. The moldering velvet, the tarnished mirrors, the dust motes hanging in the air."

"Important, I guess, if you're summoning a demon. Riley said you started to remember."

"In dribs and drabs, though I do find a certain strange attraction to the place. It's… homey."

Emma looked around at the dusty, dark, dilapidated theater. "Well, I'm just glad we're making progress. Where is everyone?"

"Oh yes, they're below. Follow me… if you dare."

Emma frowned at the demon. He looked a little too delighted with himself.

"Hey, Emma! Check this out." Riley called from behind the curtain.

"If I dare?" Emma regarded the demon suspiciously. "Is this one of your tricks?"

Just then a hand grabbed Emma's wrist and pulled her through the heavy curtain into an area filled with people and lit with portable lanterns. The owner of the hand proved to be Riley, who looked annoyed. "Al, I told you to dial it back."

"Oh please. What's the harm in having a little fun? I am *so bored*. I thought this would be *exciting*."

Riley turned to Emma. "I swear it's like having a toddler. But come look at what we found!" They led Emma to the area where Astrid and Mallory were staring at the floor and taking notes. There appeared to be yellow paint of some kind streaked on the stage in a zigzag pattern.

"Graffiti?" Emma asked. "It looks like someone took a spray can to the floor."

"Not paint," Riley said. "Sulfur. There's a ladder if you want to get the bird's-eye view. Makes it easier to see what's going on."

Emma eyed the ladder warily. She gave it a little push, and it swayed from side to side. "Are you sure this is safe?"

"We're in an abandoned theater with a chaos demon, attempting to track down the arcane practitioner who summoned him. I have *no idea* if we're safe."

"Good point." Emma started climbing. It only took a moment to get to the top. "It's not so bad up here," she called down. Then she saw exactly what had been drawn on the stage in sulfur.

She hadn't recognized it at first because the lines weren't straight. Now they came together to form a larger pattern. The zigzag lines were writing around a familiar shape.

"It's a pentagram."

"Yep, classic summoning pentagram," Riley called up to her. "Whoever made this really abides by the old school."

"What's that language?"

"Mallory is working on that. At first glance, it appears to be an archaic dialect of French." Riley waited as Emma began to descend the ladder. "What we've got here looks like the remnants of a typical European summoning ritual from the Middle Ages. Wooden floor: check. Sulfur pentagram: check. Candles: check— Hey, don't step in that!"

"What?" Emma lifted her right foot off the ground.

"I'm pretty sure that orange spot by your shoe is where the aqua regia was poured out."

"Why would they be using aqua regia?" She sniffed. Sure enough, she smelled the acrid tang of strong hydrochloric acid.

"To dissolve the gold in. What else? It's expensive as heck to summon a demon."

"I guess; otherwise everybody would be doing it."

"Professor?" Astrid called. She was staring at the floor in the middle of the pentagram. "I think you might want to take a look at this."

Emma and Riley joined Astrid. "What are we looking at?" Riley asked.

"A soft spot in the floor," Astrid told them.

"Is the wood rotten? I'd be surprised if the roof had never leaked."

Emma bent down to a squatting position and poked the

spot Astrid indicated. It didn't have the soft, spongy texture of rotten wood. "It feels like there's a spring underneath—"

Just then a pigeon flapped its wings above them. Startled, Emma lost her balance and fell forward. Her palm landed on the loose spot, and it pushed all the way in with a *click*.

Somewhere beneath them, a mechanism engaged, and the floor moved. Center stage began slowly descending, carrying Emma and Riley's team into the darkness below.

CHAPTER 31
CREEP

"Technically speaking," Riley said, "most theaters of this size will have at least one trap door in the stage. They're used to quickly get rid of props, for actors to appear out of nowhere…"

"Technically speaking… Are they all lit up by red Christmas lights?" Emma asked, studying the strings of flickering red lights stapled to the ceiling.

"I wonder where the power's coming from," Riley wondered.

"And who left the lights on," Emma said.

"And who took these pictures," Astrid added. When all eyes turned to her, she gestured to a clothesline that ran from wall to wall. On it were clipped about a dozen eight-by-ten black-and-white prints. "It's a darkroom."

Emma unclipped a print. It was damp to the touch. "Someone must have been working here recently." She squinted at the image, but it was slightly out of focus and hard to make out in the red light. She clicked on her flashlight, looked at the photo, and gasped.

She saw her own face.

"It's you?" Riley said, glancing over her shoulder. "Is that your house?"

"Yeah, it's a photo of me leaving my house yesterday morning to go to the play. I can tell from the clothes. Viv was with me, but whoever took this was only interested in me I guess." Emma took a careful breath, willing herself not to panic. When she spoke, her voice was almost too calm. "Why is there a photo of me in this creepy underground darkroom?"

The group was silent.

"Why is there a photo of me in the... demon summoner's lair? I'm going to need someone to explain this to me, because I'm about to freak out."

"Maybe he likes you," Al said, breaking the silence.

"What? Why are you looking at me like that?"

"I've found a stack of older photos," Astrid said. "Maybe they can provide some clues."

There was a photo of Emma talking with the strange man in the brown suit. There was another one of Emma emerging from Diedre's shop in a completely new outfit except for her tatty sandals. "That one is from last summer when Diedre helped me get ready for the Neighborhood Association meeting." She swallowed. "This creep has been following me around ever since I got here."

"How could he do it without being seen?" Riley asked. "It doesn't make sense."

"We're talking about someone who summoned an actual living, breathing demon from the netherworld—"

"Nether regions," Al corrected.

"I'm not going to say that. Anyway, he summoned a demon from... the demon place. Taking a few photos should be a walk in the park for that kind of guy."

"Oh my gods, take a look at this," Riley said, passing a photo to Emma—a grainy black-and-white taken with a telephoto lens. The subject was an old psychic shop. In front of it, Emma's late aunt Cora looked as if she were leaving to run an errand. It would have been a completely normal photo if it hadn't been for one detail: *Coralee was looking directly into the camera.*

Emma stared at the photo for a moment, stunned. Then she spoke. "I doubt she could have seen him from such a distance, but maybe she knew he was there. One of her spirit guides could have told her."

"Whoever this guy is, he is playing a long game. What a creep," Riley said in disgust.

"I hate to break it to y'all," Astrid said from the other end of the room, "but it gets weirder." She bent over and picked up a small sack-like object crudely stitched together out of burlap. It had four feet and a long tail.

Riley took the object and examined it. "So this guy makes creepy stuffed animals on the side when he's not busy stalking Emma. Classy."

Emma stared at the thing. She finally spoke, almost to herself. "It's a rat."

"Of course this brings to mind several traditions of imbuing inanimate—"

Emma's mind drifted away from the present, back to the night she'd been alone in the core. She was sitting by the dried-up fountain when the rats appeared, first on the rooftops and then in the streets...

She remembered being chased through a darkened building by thousands of the creatures—thousands of shining eyes in the dark. *But those animals were real flesh and blood—weren't they?*

She remembered how they scrambled up her legs.

She remembered how they climbed down the wall like spiders.

Riley was still talking. Emma knew that because their

mouth was moving, but she couldn't hear. The words simply didn't register in her ears. Instead, she heard a sound like wind rushing, like water raging. She saw that from the burlap rat's neck there poured a thin stream of fine white sand.

CHAPTER 32
LIBRARY

"What does this mean?" Emma blurted as she stumbled back into the moment and stared at the *thing* still in Riley's hand.

"Your guess is as good as mine. Though it's starting to feel like somebody has it out for you. For your whole family."

"I'm so sick of this!" Emma shouted, surprising even herself. "Why can't I just live in my stupid house and apply for stupid jobs and fix my stupid plumbing? I didn't ask for any of this. It's not fair."

The room was silent, and then Riley spoke. "No, it's not fair."

"Most certainly," Al butted in. "It's not fair that everyone doesn't get to have this much excitement and drama in their puny little lives."

"Now's not the time," Riley snapped.

"They so rarely get to even smell—let alone taste—a life lived to its fullest."

"Shut up, Al!"

"What? I was empathizing. Isn't that what you people do?"

"I think you need a little more practice," Emma said, the

corners of her mouth lifting ever so slightly upward. "Sorry, guys. This has all been a little overwhelming."

"To put it mildly," Riley agreed.

"So where do we go from here?"

It was Astrid who answered, eyes twinkling with mischief. "Maybe we should try the door?"

Everyone in the group began craning their necks, looking around for the door that she mentioned. Finally, Riley broke the silence. "I give up. What door?"

"Over here. Do you feel the breeze?"

"It's coming from the wall, but the wall is solid brick." Riley raked the beam of their flashlight across the wall's surface. The light revealed two cracks a few feet apart running from the floor up to the ceiling. They pushed on it. The wall opened inward.

"Of course this place would have secret doors," Emma muttered. "It's a tunnel. Shame there's no light— Hey, look at this!" She pointed at the dusty floor. "Footprints."

"All in favor of entering the scary tunnel?" Riley asked. Everyone raised their hand.

Well, almost everyone.

"I have no desire to enter into the scary tunnel," Al said. He wrinkled his nose, as if he was smelling something unpleasant.

"Al...," Riley said in the tone parents use when they reach the end of their rope. "Is this another one of your tricks?"

"Tricks? Me? No! I merely wish to become more acquainted with this theater. If I wish to tread the boards one day, I'll need to know her like I know the back of my own hand."

"Are you going to run away?"

"No! I give you my word."

"As a chaos demon."

Mallory looked up from her notebook where she'd been

diligently recording everything that happened. "I'll stay with him."

"You're sure?" Riley asked. "He's kind of a handful. Okay, it's your funeral. Ready, everyone? Forward into the unknown!" They stepped into the tunnel.

"I think the unknown could use a housekeeper," Emma said as she walked through the darkness, kicking chip bags and soda cans out of her path. She sniffed. "Maybe a mold assessment too." The very idea of a secret tunnel was starting to grate on Emma. She didn't know anything about it, and she hated not knowing things.

"I wonder where all these other tunnels go," Astrid said, shining her flashlight into an opening in the wall. The beam was swallowed by the darkness.

"It's a good thing this place is such a mess. Otherwise, we wouldn't have footprints in the dust to follow."

"Why'd you have to say that, Riley?"

"What?"

"You're a professor of applied *folklore,* for crying out loud. You should know that as soon as you say it's a good thing there are footprints out loud it's only a matter of time—"

"Before the footprints go away." Riley stopped and stared at the floor, searching with her flashlight beam. "I hate to break it to you guys, but there are no more footprints."

"Is it me, or is this part somehow cleaner?" Emma said. "It's okay; we'll just keep going."

"We can't. The tunnel forks just ahead." Riley used their flashlight to point out the two paths, one leading left, the other right. "Maybe you could ask the spirit guides?"

Emma was suddenly glad for the darkness because her face went red. "I don't... really have any."

"But you said your aunt—"

"Yes, *my aunt* could do that sort of thing. Maybe I could too, if I had someone to teach me, but all I've got are a few undead friends and a random lady in a dirty wedding dress that just kind of... stares."

"Maybe if you think about her, she'll come?"

"Why do you think *she'd* even know the way? But whatever; I'll try."

Emma pulled up an image of Miss Havisham in her mind, focusing all her attention on remembering every detail: her tattered dress, the way she hung in the air, her strangely... empty face.

She opened her eyes and winced as a pang of guilt passed through her heart. "I'm sorry; nothing's happening."

"In that case, we'll revert to the backup plan."

"We have a backup plan?"

"Totally. Now does anyone have a coin?"

"Mrow!" The sound came from behind them, and one green eye and one yellow one peered out of the darkness.

"Captain?" Emma said. "What are you doing here?"

The cat stared at them all for a moment before turning tail and walking into the path on the left. He flicked his tail as if commanding them to follow.

"Could that be Al playing another trick on us?" Riley wondered aloud.

"No. When Al impersonated the captain, he was a lot nicer." The captain hissed as Emma said the demon's name. "See what I mean?" she asked as she followed the cat into the tunnel on the left.

"I wonder how long he's known about these tunnels," Riley mused.

"He and the other cats in the night watch do have a habit of mysteriously appearing at the right place. Maybe they use the tunnels to get around."

"For that to be the case, they'd have to branch out under the entire neighborhood."

"We *have* been walking for a while. There's no way we're still under the theater."

The tunnel came to an end at an ordinary-looking steel door. It opened into a narrow stairwell painted an institutional shade of gray. Metal stairs led up.

The door at the top of the stairs led, unexpectedly, into a janitor's closet that opened into a forest of empty bookshelves. On the floor around them were books, neatly piled and waiting to be reshelved.

"The library?" Riley asked.

"No, it can't be," Emma replied. "I was in the library yesterday morning. It was a disaster area. All the books were trashed."

But as they emerged from the stacks, Emma realized it was true. She saw the reference desk in the corner, and then she looked at the broad tables where she'd sat with Alice Beyer's spirit. "I was here just yesterday," she said again, confused. "Every single book had been destroyed. The pages were ripped out, and they were all on the floor. You could barely walk!"

"I guess somebody decided to clean them up and bring in new books?"

"Maybe. It's just—"

The captain jumped up on a desk and sniffed the air from all directions. He let out a low growl, and his hair stood on end, making him look even larger and more intimidating.

"Maybe it's the summoner's doing?"

"It'd have to be a real sorcerer's-apprentice operation."

The captain lost the scent of whatever had disturbed him. He sat and, after eyeing the darkness warily, began cleaning himself.

Next to him on the table was a pile of old yellowing newspapers. Emma examined it with her flashlight. "The *Undertown Tattler*! Dash told me about this. It was the old newspaper!"

"Those are going to disintegrate the moment you pick

them up. It looks like someone was compiling them into books."

"Dash asked me to find this sort of thing to help him recover his memory. Shoot, when did he say he was born? I think it was around 1900."

"Wouldn't it be more useful to know when he died?"

"He doesn't remember. But based on the way he acts, I'd guess it was the late 1920s."

Riley searched the completed books. "Here are the volumes for 1929 and 1930. Did he die during the Great Depression?"

"I don't know; he's not able to remember a lot. Do you think it would be okay for me to borrow the books?"

Riley shrugged. "It's a library. I suppose it's fine, as long as you bring them back." Then Riley's face went blank. "A library... Oh my god, Emma, I think I know where to find the Reinhold files!"

"Is it another creepy place? I've had all I can stand for tonight."

"It's a computer thing. We can do it at your house."

"Thank goodness," Emma said, taking the two large, leather-bound volumes of the *Undertown Tattler* and holding them against her chest. The captain jumped off the table, leading them to the library's front door and down the steps into the inky darkness. As they walked, a crow cawed far away.

CHAPTER 33
MIDNIGHT OIL

Emma removed the tea bags from two steaming mugs and carried them to the kitchen table. Riley was there, staring intently at their computer. "I hope mint is okay. Diedre made it from her herb garden. It's pretty good."

"I'm connecting to the university network. Did you realize that your connection is incredibly slow?"

"Yeah," Emma said, stifling a yawn. She took a sip of tea and felt the warmth revive her. "I'm lucky to have any internet service at all with the way things have been going around here." She glanced toward her dining room, which *still* needed repairs before she could host Thanksgiving. "You couldn't find the Reinhold documents before. What makes you so sure you can find them now?"

"Earlier, I was looking for them in our document management system. That's where we have your aunt's case files digitized, categorized, and indexed." Riley paused to type something in, then turned to Emma. "Why aren't they there?"

"Maybe your students forgot to upload them?"

"Or someone deleted them from the system."

"But who—?"

"It doesn't matter right now. When we were at the library, I remembered that I have an archive of the raw document images stashed in a read-only repository."

"So it would be impossible for someone to delete the Reinhold file."

"Exactly. These are just images. They're not searchable. But if we look through all of them—"

"All of them? How many are there?"

"Just a sec...," Riley said, voice trailing off. "Ten thousand three hundred and seventy-two."

Emma looked hard at Riley. "You're serious. Well, in that case, I'd better fix a whole pot of tea."

"We can switch off every hundred images; that way our eyes don't get too bleary. I imagine it should only take an hour or two. It's a shame Viv isn't here to help."

"She's on a date," Emma said as she sipped her tea. "She told me all about it when we were... investigating the community center."

"Really? Who's the date with?" Riley picked up their mug of tea and took an inquisitive sip.

"I'm not sure. I think she's a topsider. They were going to meet in Cap Hill and walk to the movies."

"Surprising..." Riley glanced at Emma, raised an eyebrow, and grinned.

"What? Why are you looking at me like that?"

"No reason. It's just been a few years since she's dated. Her last relationship really put her through the ringer. Besides," Riley grinned, "she spends all her free time over here helping you with the house. Do you want to go first, or should I?"

"What? Oh, looking through the scans? I'll go first." Emma sat and began flipping through the images. It was boring work, and her mind began to wander.

"I never got a chance to look up Reinhold. What kind of business is it?"

"A little bit of everything. My dad worked for them in the eighties when they were a small aerospace firm making bolts for the space shuttle. A few years ago, new management came in, and they started branching out into parts for planes, then cars, then phones, oil, and real estate."

"You sound like a brochure."

"Again, my dad. So is it time to switch off?"

"Yeah, I'm getting cross-eyed." Emma ceded the computer to Riley. As time passed, they traded places a few more times. On her breaks, Emma picked up the *Scientific American* on the counter and started reading an article about a physics principal called the conservation of information.

A moment later, she was back at the computer, flipping through the scans. She paused and called to Riley, "Hey! I've got a page with Reinhold at the top. There's... at least a dozen of them."

"Really? What do they say?" Riley asked, walking over to the table.

Emma began to read aloud. "'Met with client, Darla Reinhold...'"

"What's up? Why'd you stop?"

"'Darla Reinhold, twenty years of age.' Could that be the same Darla who lives on Easthill? She's on the board of the Neighborhood Association. Gladys told me we had a Reinhold in the neighborhood, but she wouldn't tell me who it was! Of course she'd protect a fellow member of the board."

"What does the file say about her? Why did she see your aunt?"

"She was being haunted by some kind of spirit," Emma summarized as she scanned the text for the important parts. "She thought it might be her grandmother, who was a real hard case. Aunt Cora contacted the spirit, and... it actually was the grandmother!"

"What are the odds?"

"She was hopping mad about the man Darla was seeing

and— Wow, Grandma was racist." Emma leaned back, frowning. "It just kind of ends there."

"Did the grandmother ever leave her alone?"

"It doesn't say."

"Is there any information in there that could confirm that Darla Reinhold is the Darla on Easthill?"

"Let me see," Emma said, flipping back through the scanned documents. "No, their ages roughly line up, but there's nothing definitive. I think I have to go talk with her."

"Now?" Riley said, yawning. "It's almost midnight."

"She'll be too tired to lie to me. Besides, if she's not awake, I can always go back tomorrow."

A message popped up on Riley's computer. They leaned in to read it. "As much as I'd love to join you, it looks like Al's turning into a pumpkin. I need to go relieve Astrid and Mallory," Riley said, frowning. "I also need to talk to them about how this file went missing."

Riley stood, took a gulp of tea, and was off. Emma once again found herself alone.

The clock on the wall ticked. It really was almost midnight. Fatigue snuggled into her muscles, but there was no chance of sleep. She'd be tossing and turning all night, wondering about Darla.

Darla Reinhold. No wonder the woman had such a fancy house. She was part of one of the richest families in the country.

One thing was for sure: Darla was wrapped up in all this more than she'd let on. The Reinhold account looked like it was central to both murders. Harold's firm helped them cook the books. The man in the brown suit was their employee.

Before she knew it, Emma had her raincoat on and was heading out the door into the night. The rain had picked up, and she regarded it for a moment before she pulled on her hood and walked, almost slipping, down her wet steps.

CHAPTER 34
UNMASKED

The night brought a mist, which hovered in the air. It made a halo around her flashlight as she walked quickly across the street and onto the green of Undertown Square.

Emma thought it had been dark before, but it was nothing compared to this. The clouds blocked the moon, and all she could see now was the nimbus of light in front of her. Still, she walked the way easily now because she knew it.

She tried desperately not to think of the mysterious person they'd pursued in the tunnels under the theater—the person who had taken so many photos of her. She unconsciously quickened her pace.

When she reached Main, she breathed a sigh of relief. Here the streetlights actually worked. She could see her surroundings, for once, and was able to switch off the flashlight.

The hill to Darla's house seemed easier this time… or perhaps she was just more motivated. Emma had to know what the old woman's role was in all this.

That made her stop in her tracks.

How did she expect to extract that information from her?

Walk up and ask? Maybe. People usually told the truth even if they didn't mean to.

The house was dark when she reached the front door, but the sign by the mailbox read MILLER RESIDENCE. She pressed the button and heard a doorbell ring inside.

A moment later, she saw a light come on. Then the sound of shuffling feet, and a small curtain pulled aside.

There were the sounds of a lock being turned, and the door swung open to reveal Darla. She was wearing a silk nightgown with a Japanese print along with a crimson silk bonnet.

"Emma? What are you doing here at this time of night?"

"I was researching the case, and I needed to ask—"

"Oh, hush up, and get yourself in here out of the rain," Darla said, opening the door and letting Emma come in. "Young people today have got no sense, going about at all times of night in all kinds of weather."

Emma allowed herself to be ushered in and let Darla take her sopping raincoat. "You see… I…" She found that looking at the woman there in her fine dressing gown, oozing with dignity in a way that frankly made her jealous, the words didn't come like she'd imagined the scenario playing out.

"Well, out with it. And you might as well sit down. I wasn't really asleep anyway," she said, ushering Emma to a leather sectional located in a sunken seating area. "I sit up reading most the night. Comes with age, I guess."

"I've… been looking into the murders. You told me you didn't think that Clarence did it. Well, things are a lot more complicated than I ever would have imagined."

"How so?"

"Well, you see, it turns out that the chairman's firm was involved in some shady accounting for Reinhold Industries." Emma watched the woman carefully to see how she reacted to the name.

She grinned. "And you thought since I'm a Reinhold that I must have had something to do with it."

"Not exactly—"

"So you got all excited and rushed up here to interrogate me. That's the real reason you're here so late, isn't it?"

"I… It doesn't sound very nice when you put it that way."

"The world isn't a nice place. It's time you figured that out, especially if you're going to be running around playing amateur detective." Darla sighed and rolled her eyes. "Did you see my name on my mailbox?"

"Miller."

"Yes, Miller. Did you notice what it didn't say? Reinhold. Does that tell you anything?"

"That you're… hiding something?"

"Wow, you just come right out and say whatever you're thinking, don't you? *No*, it tells you that I'm not a Reinhold. At least not anymore." She sighed, then looked out the large picture window onto the neighborhood's lights twinkling below. "My family, they're not good people. When I married Teddy, they disowned me."

"Teddy's your husband?"

"May he rest in peace. My parents couldn't abide me marrying a Black man. I think they expected me to marry some captain of industry, to seal an alliance or some such nonsense. Can you imagine?"

"That doesn't sound very human."

"Frankly, to run a business the size of theirs, you have to become something that's not quite human. But what goes around comes around. My family's all been pushed out. My brothers lost control over the company a decade ago."

"Would you be surprised to learn that there was a Reinhold employee making a survey of all the vacant properties in the core?"

"At this point in life, Emma, nothing surprises me. Of course I have no connection with this man."

"He was killed, pushed out Clarice's upstairs window."

"That saddens me a little, as any death would sadden me, though I don't know what it has to do with *me*. Now if you'll excuse me, I'll be getting back to my novel." She stood and waited for Emma to stand.

But Emma was distracted by the ghastly figure that had just appeared. "Miss Havisham?" she whispered. The specter's veil was covering its face. The long train of its frayed wedding dress floated behind it, blown by an unnatural breeze.

It moved. Emma followed it.

"Where do you think you're going?" Darla called out as Emma followed Miss Havisham past the open-concept kitchen, up the stairs, and onto a landing that overlooked the grand living room. They stopped in front of a door, which Emma opened.

A woman tumbled out. After jumping to her feet, the woman backed away and pressed against the wall like Emma was the most frightening person she'd ever seen.

She had blond hair in a messy bun, and she wore an oversized Yale sweatshirt. Her face was streaked with tears.

"Clarice!" Emma said.

"They really killed him? Are you sure? They killed Paul?"

CHAPTER 35
FUGITIVE

The three of them sat around Darla's kitchen table with hot mugs of decaf tea. Clarice's was heavily doctored with milk and sugar.

"I… just can't believe they killed him," Clarice said. She sat with her legs up on the chair, her sweatshirt pulled over them.

"The man in the brown suit was named Paul? You know him then."

"We were working together."

"For Reinhold Industries?"

"For Reinhold, yes. I…"

"You were involved with the accounting irregularities, weren't you?"

"I… didn't want to be. I was trying to fix things. Paul and I were working together." She looked away and scowled as if remembering something unpleasant. "We thought we could score a coup and put things right before anyone noticed the irregularities." She suddenly looked up. "It was all Harold's idea. I didn't kill him, but I'm glad he's dead."

"What, exactly, was Harold's idea?"

"He was the original owner of the Reinhold account. It

wasn't normal, you know, for the head partner to be directly in charge of an account like that, but for such a prestigious name, they wanted to give them the star treatment. But Harold was incompetent. He made me do all his dirty work."

"Made you?"

"He had information about me that couldn't get out. At the Christmas party—" She turned away in disgust.

"You had a relationship with Harold."

"If you want to call it that. Clarence and I were going through a rough time. We separated—trying it on for size. Things were bad after our son died."

Emma swallowed thinking of the untouched room she'd rummaged through at their house. *It looked like he just moved away for college.*

"We drifted apart. Then… we drifted back together," she said and flashed a shy smile.

"Harold blackmailed you into committing fraud on the Reinhold account."

"The new CEO of the company had lost a bunch of money branching into lots of different industries they knew nothing about. But all the losses were tied up in subsidiary entities. Reinhold realized that if they had these subsidiaries do deals with each other in a certain way, they could make it look like the whole thing made a profit. We were an independent auditor. Harold found the fraud. They convinced him to play ball and cover it up. I thought I could do one better. I thought I could turn it around."

Emma leaned back in the chair, trying to digest everything she'd heard. "I don't understand where the man in the brown suit—Paul—enters the picture. He was making a list of vacant properties."

"The core was inaccessible for so long that the properties had no real value. Their owners wrote them off, moved away, passed them down." She picked up her coffee with shaking hands and took a sip. "Those of us living in the neighborhood know that it's only a matter of time before the core is revitalized, but that knowledge hasn't traveled far. It's a classic arbitrage opportunity."

"Reinhold wants to buy the core and... flip it?"

She flashed a shaky smile. "Seattle has some of the most expensive real estate in the country. Once it's restored, the real estate in the core is going to be worth billions of dollars."

"Which is more than enough money to fill Reinhold's coffers and ensure that the accounting irregularities go undetected." Emma frowned. "You'd sell off the center of Undertown to the highest bidder. It's hard enough for normal people to afford a place to live. You were going to make it harder."

Clarice shrugged. "I'm not proud of what I did, but we were in hot water. Desperate times call for desperate measures. Besides, if we didn't do it, someone else would have. Those properties are selling for pennies on the dollar, and it's only a matter of time before the twenty-first century catches up to this place."

What had Darla said? To be in business at the highest levels you had to turn into something that wasn't quite human. She remembered the man in the brown suit. "Did Paul work for your accounting firm?"

"He was a private investigator. We didn't want it getting around that Reinhold was making inquiries. That alone would make prices go up. I still can't believe he was murdered."

"Not only was he murdered, you're suspect number one."

"Me?" She jerked her head left, then right, like she expected to find a way out of the trap she was in. "Why on earth would I murder Paul? We were working together."

"I don't know, but the optics are bad. You vanish, leaving evidence that you fled your house in a hurry. Soon after, Paul is found dead on your front lawn, pushed out a window. The police are looking for you."

"I ran away because I was scared for my life! I received an awful letter—anonymous of course. It accused me of killing Harold. Whoever wrote it knew about our secret. They said if I didn't leave town, they would go to the police. I was more worried I would be the next one to end up dead."

The only sound in the room was the refrigerator humming and the barely audible buzz of the light fixture. Emma leaned forward in her chair. "Do you have the letter?"

"No, I burned it in the fireplace—probably a stupid decision, but I was scared to death. Darla is an old friend." She smiled at the old woman.

"You should know that the cat's out of the bag. The Reinhold scandal is going to be public knowledge soon. I imagine that your affair with Harold will be as well."

"I know; that's why I told you."

"Then tell me one more thing. Did you have anything to do with Harold's murder?"

"I almost wish I did. If it hadn't been for him, I never would have wound up in this mess. But no, I wasn't even there." The lights in the room flickered, but Clarice didn't seem to notice. "After I wished Clarence good luck, I sneaked back to the office. It was the only time I could guarantee—"

The lights went out. The refrigerator stopped humming. The three women sat in absolute silence for a long moment. Then the front door splintered and exploded inward. Suddenly, the room was filled with uniformed men with weapons drawn.

CHAPTER 36
HEAT

The three women sat on the sofa, handcuffed, while the police swarmed the house, throwing open doors and shouting, looking for God knew what. Emma's nose itched. She tried to scratch it, but the steel cuffs bit into her wrists.

The police finished their search, and the lights came back on. A tired-looking man in a rumpled button-down shirt and gray chinos walked in, pointing two uniformed officers to something in the hall.

He approached the women. "All right, let's see who we have here—"

"How *dare* you burst into my house like this and handcuff me like some criminal?" Darla spat out. "Show me your name and badge number. I'm going to speak with your superiors."

"Name's Jackson," he said, flashing his badge. "And you should know that harboring a fugitive *is* a crime, especially when murder is involved."

"A fugitive? I was merely having tea with my *friend*, who just had a terrible scare."

Clarice turned to Darla. "You shouldn't say anything else."

"You're right. I'll let Mr. Gruber handle the matter. I assume you know the name."

Emma knew the name. John Gruber was a particularly bombastic lawyer who had "helped" Emma with her house. Could he get her out of this? She frowned. This was the *last time* she'd ever try to help anyone.

"Sergeant, take these two away for processing. Now what's your name?"

Emma watched men in uniform lead Darla and Clarice away. It took Emma a moment to realize that she had been addressed. "My name is Emma Day."

"Excellent," he said. "I just had to confirm that you were who I thought you were." He waited until Darla and Clarice were out of the room, then he pulled a key from his pocket and unlocked her cuffs. "Good work, by the way."

As Emma rubbed her wrists, she felt a strange combination of gratitude and anger welling up in her chest. "Good work? What the heck do you mean, good work?"

"We knew that you were sticking your nose where it didn't belong, so we kept an eye on you. I never would have guessed Clarice would be up here."

"You followed me?"

The man shrugged. "We do what it takes to catch the bad guys. Here's a little advice: if you don't want us to know about something, don't discuss it on the phone with a prisoner."

"You taped the call." Emma frowned, trying to remember what else she'd said. "I think Clarice is innocent."

"Do innocent people run?" he said, opening a small notebook and checking an item off a list.

"You can never know how people will react when they're in a life-or-death situation. Clarice was scared."

The man looked up from his notebook. "That's for the court to decide now. You're free to go."

"You're just going to ignore me." Her anger was overshadowing the gratitude.

"Did I say you're free to go? What I meant was, you *have* to go. Now."

Emma's face was red as she took her raincoat and stormed out of the house. *Darla was right. How dare they!*

———

"Emma, hold up," a man called from the dark. As he walked into the light, she saw that it was Marcus.

"Don't tell me you were having me followed too."

He held up his hands. "I didn't do it. I'm not a cop —remember?"

"Then why are you here?"

"I'm the neighborhood liaison. Whenever the county sheriff shows up, I'm supposed to come keep an eye on them." He stifled a yawn. "I just wish they would have waited until morning."

"Well, it's over, so you can go back to bed. They arrested Darla and Clarice. I tried to tell that detective he was making a mistake, but he ignored me."

"Arrested them, huh?"

"I thought they were about to arrest me too."

Marcus paused, trying to find the right words. "Emma, two people are dead. Three people—all prominent, wealthy community members—have been arrested."

"I know! It's so infuriating. I tried to tell that man, but he ignored me!"

"That man is a *detective*. He works for the *state*. Do you understand where I'm going with this?"

"No."

Marcus sighed and shook his head. "There are certain groups of people who don't have to worry too much about the powers-that-be. They can play with fire all day long and never get burned because society protects them. You're one of those people."

"What? That's crazy."

"Is it? Didn't the cops just let you go?"

"Yeah, but that's because they were watching me, and they knew I wasn't involved."

"Look around you, girl! People with more power and money than you'll ever have are getting killed and locked up. You're free now because they gave you the benefit of the doubt. What if one day they don't?"

Emma was silent as she looked down at the lights of Undertown, feeling the mist that blew against her face. "You're saying that I should stop causing trouble."

"A minute ago, you were mad about the detective ignoring you. I'm saying you should take some time and think about what would happen if people started paying attention." He looked into the distance and sighed. "You're a grown woman. You can make your own decisions. I just want to make sure you understand the consequences."

"Thanks, I guess," Emma said and smiled. She glanced down at Marcus's rumpled shirt, then at the black hair beginning to go gray and wrinkles around his eyes. "I feel like I just got scolded by my dad or something."

He chuckled. "I'm not your dad, but you do remind me of someone I knew a long time ago."

"I think I understand your point, but it's hard for me to let things go when they don't make sense. They gnaw at me."

"Reminds me of an old saying about a curious cat. Just be careful."

Emma turned and began walking down the steep concrete steps. The detective's words echoed in her head: *Good work.* As she descended into the dark wooded trail, realization descended on her. Despite all her efforts—no, *because of* all her efforts—two more people were in jail.

It's my fault, Emma thought.

CHAPTER 37
DAMAGE

Emma's heart was in her stomach as she trudged across the inky green. Exhaustion, held at bay by the night's excitement, descended upon her as she hauled herself up the front steps and unlocked her front door.

"Mrow!" The captain greeted her as she turned on the hallway light. Emma looked at him and did a double take. He was soaking wet! His luxuriant mane of black-and-brown fur was matted down and dripping.

"What happened to you?" she asked. Then she heard the hiss. "Oh no! Not again!"

She raced to the dining room. Water misted her face as it sprayed from the ceiling onto the new drywall and collected in a pool on the floor. Somewhere in the ceiling, the old pipes had sprung yet another leak. Above her, a sheet of drywall buckled under the weight and collapsed, sending several gallons of water onto Emma's head.

She cursed, wiping the water from her face, then made her way to the basement where she used a large wrench to turn off the house's water main.

Back in the dining room, she surveyed the damage. All the work that she and Viv had done was ruined.

It was time to face the facts. She was never going to get the dining room cleaned up in time to host Thanksgiving. She was never going to find the murderer. She was never going to have a normal life with normal friends and a normal job.

She went to the kitchen and took a mug off the shelf. The kettle was empty, so she took it to the sink, but when she turned the faucet handle, nothing happened. *Oh yeah.*

She continued back to the laundry room, where she traded her soaking-wet clothes for fresh pajamas, fully intending to collapse into bed, but as she rounded the corner to the stairs, something caught her eye. On a small table near the front door, she saw the *Undertown Tattler* archives she'd borrowed from the library.

At least I can help Dash, Emma thought. She grabbed the books on her way to her bedroom. Finally in bed, she pulled the covers close and began to thumb through the issues of the old paper.

It was truly a local paper. Most of the articles were about normal people in the community doing things. A local amateur baseball team went to state. A bank opened. They finished construction on the library.

She turned the page and saw a headline that piqued her curiosity: "David Meyers Still Missing." *Hadn't Dash mentioned a friend named Davy?* The man had been staying with his parents but had disappeared overnight. His bed hadn't been slept in.

She turned the page and saw another headline: "David Meyers Presumed Dead." *Maybe that's the unfinished business Dash needs to resolve before he can move on.*

She turned the page again, but what she saw made her blood run cold. The headline simply read: "Dashiell Gruber Arrested For Meyers Killing."

Could Dash be a murderer?

It didn't make sense. Dash was one of the nicest guys she

knew, living or dead. Sure, he could be mopey sometimes, but who didn't mope from time to time?

She turned back to the article. It was short, consisting of just a few lines without any additional details. She flipped through the rest of the book, but there was no additional information.

She'd need to go back to the library and get the next year's issues of the *Tattler* to see what happened. *Oh Lord,* she'd need to figure out what to tell to Dash. It was clear he didn't remember any of this.

Setting the book aside, she lay in bed, staring into the distance. She stayed there, mind spinning, until the weight of the world pressed down on her and crushed her into sleep.

CHAPTER 38
WARM SHOULDER

Emma awoke in midair, blanket twisted around her feet. She hit the floor with a *thud* and stared uncomprehendingly at the sunlit room. Downstairs, there was a pounding on the door.

She scrambled out of bed and checked herself in the mirror. Plaster dust: check. Yesterday's makeup: check. Bedhead: check. *Time for another day.*

She grabbed a ponytail holder, twisting her hair into a messy bun. Then she found a pair of jeans, sniffed them, and put them on. Her heart sank as she remembered the previous night.

"Just a minute!" she yelled, hopping on one foot while she pulled a sock onto the other. *There.* She glanced in the mirror. She was the spitting image of a grown woman whose life was *definitely* not falling apart at the seams.

Running downstairs, she opened the door. Viv stood on her porch, wearing a worried expression. "Is everything okay, Emma?"

Emma looked down at her clothes, "Do I look that bad?"

"No, it's just— What's that smell? It's like mildew."

"Oh my goodness, I didn't clean up any of the water

before I went to bed. I'm such an idiot! Come on in, I'll show you. I'm afraid I can't offer you any breakfast."

"Em, it's two in the afternoon. That's why I came over. Nobody had seen you, and you didn't answer your phone."

"Jeez, I guess I needed to sleep. I had a long night." She led Viv to the dining room, which was somehow even worse than she remembered it. Most of the ceiling was on the floor, and the walls were covered in large dark water stains.

"That's no joke. What happened?" Viv walked into the room and surveyed the wreckage.

"I was out when the pipe burst. I'm not sure how long it was flooding—long enough, I guess. I'm starting to wonder if I'm cut out to be a homeowner. How was your date?"

"What? Oh, it was nice."

"I wish something nice would happen to me for once. I'll tell you what. I'm done with this whole *murder* thing. I give up."

Viv looked at her, concerned. "I guess something really got to you, huh?"

"That's putting it mildly. The freaking cops were listening in on my conversations with Clarence. They followed me to Darla's house last night and *arrested* Darla and Clarice."

"Did you think she was guilty?"

"I *did*, but then I talked with her. Everything's so much more complex that I thought. The truth is I don't have a clue."

"Do you at least have a garbage bag? I'll help you pick this up."

"Yeah, thanks," Emma said. She disappeared for a moment, then came back with a large plastic trash bag. She bent down and, with Viv's help, began filling it with debris. "And I haven't even told you the worst thing of all."

"You haven't?"

"Dash wanted me to help him research his life so that he could recover his memory and pass through the veil."

"Did you find something about him in your aunt's files?"

Viv asked as she folded a piece of soggy drywall in half and stuffed it in the bag.

"No, I found it in the library. I don't really understand *how*, but someone's restoring it. I found an article saying he was arrested for the murder of his best friend!"

"*Shut up!* Are you serious?"

"What am I supposed to tell him when he asks how my research is going? 'Oh yeah, by the way, you killed your best friend?'"

"You only know that he was arrested. He might have been innocent."

"I don't think it matters. He has a habit of… disappearing when he starts to remember things. If I even told him he was arrested, he'll flip out. I might not see him for months or years."

"Then don't tell him."

"How could I—?"

"Emma, it's not your responsibility to tell him—especially if you think it'll do damage."

"But he's my friend. I promised him I would take care of this for him. If I don't—"

"Can you listen to yourself for a second? Can't you see how hard you're being on yourself? Dash is your friend, but it's not your job to fix him," Viv said, pausing her work and facing Emma. "By the way, it's also not your job to solve every murder that happens in Undertown—or to host a perfect Thanksgiving dinner."

"But if I don't have Thanksgiving, my mom will never leave me alone," she said, flinging debris into the bag. "If I don't solve the murder, an innocent guy could go to prison. And if I don't help Dash, he'll be stuck on this side of the veil forever." Emma stood and stomped into the kitchen. Viv followed her.

"Yeah, maybe."

"What?" Emma looked up, confused.

"I said: maybe. Maybe Dash will be stuck here. Or he'll be miserable. Maybe he did kill that guy, and when he finally remembers, he'll freak out and disappear for a hundred years."

"And those would be bad things."

"Maybe they would be, but it's not your job to keep them from happening."

"It isn't?"

"No!"

"I need to take care of my friends though. It's… good to take care of your friends."

"Yeah, but it's a balancing act—not one or the other. Real friends don't want you to give up your own life to fix their problems."

"What *do* real friends want?"

"You!" Viv blurted. "You don't have to *do* things to have friends. It's the same with everything else. You don't have to pull off a perfect Thanksgiving to deserve your mom's respect. You don't have to solve every crime in Undertown to live here. You get to have a life."

"I do?" Emma understood the words Viv was saying, but they just didn't seem very true.

"You are Emma freaking Day! You talk with ghosts!" Viv grabbed an issue of *Scientific American* from the counter and waived it in the air. "You do smart science stuff I don't understand. You bought an amazing house on your own and are restoring it. You're kind of a badass, and I'm proud to be your friend. Heck, I would be even if you didn't do *any* of that stuff."

Emma blushed and looked down. "That's maybe the nicest thing anyone's ever said to me." She looked up, smiling.

"Yeah?" She playfully boxed Emma's shoulder. "Don't let it go to your head. So, uh, I think we've made a pretty good start on the cleanup. I've got a dehumidifier and some fans back at the coffee shop. We can swing by and get them if you want."

"You're sure that wouldn't be too much trouble?"

"It's okay to let people help you."

Emma was quiet for a long moment while she let the words sink in. Then she rushed to Viv and gave the taller woman a tight hug. "Let's get those fans."

CHAPTER 39
BIGGEST FAN

The afternoon air was crisp and smelled like cinnamon. Emma and Viv walked past the library and theater to Deadtown Coffee.

Nothing had really changed since last night. The murders were still unsolved. Her dining room was still ruined. Dash was still a riddle. But somehow, in her heart, she knew that everything had changed.

Yesterday, she was overwhelmed. It felt like she was putting together a puzzle with too many pieces. But now she knew the opposite was true: a piece was missing. Once she found it, everything else would slip right into place.

Deadtown was empty except for Laney, the barista, leaning against the counter reading a romance novel. She glanced up at them and gestured to the curtained door. "You're late. Party's in the back."

"We're just dropping in to grab a few things. Emma's house is having an identity crisis. It wants to be an aquarium."

"Very funny," Emma said, punching Viv on the shoulder.

In the back room, Viv disappeared into a storage closet. Emma found the theater crew sitting on the couch and arguing about the practicality of restaging their performance of *Julius Caesar* in the old theater.

Dash sat contentedly in the corner, waiting for the discussion to veer toward lighting and atmospherics. Emma felt a pang of guilt as he gave her a little wave.

Riley, who was not able to see Dash, interrupted. "We decided that we owed it to the neighborhood to give them another chance to see the show since the last performance was interrupted," Riley explained. "Al thinks we should stage it in the old theater even though it's not restored at all—"

"Think of the *drama*," Al said, twinkling his fingers. "The audience in darkness, the stage lit by candles and the other-worldly glow of the undead."

"We'd need more stagehands," Astrid said. "I could ask my brother."

Al scoffed. "I'll never understand how you humans can be in the same room as your siblings."

"Sometimes we can't," Riley quipped.

"All righty, Em. I'll carry the dehumidifier if you carry the fans," Viv said as she emerged from the closet.

Emma picked up the two dented box fans, then turned to the theater crew. "Hey, when is the performance? I don't want to miss it, especially if it's in that creepy old theater."

"I'll let you know once we decide," Riley said. "We could do it any time once we decide to."

"That's quick. I would have imagined it'd take more time to regroup."

"He may not look like it, but Al's a quick study, and his shape-shifting ability means he can perform more than one role."

———

The smell of mildew greeted them when they returned to Emma's house.

"We'll open the windows, get the fans blowing, and it'll be dry in no time," Viv said.

"I hope you're right. I guess Thanksgiving is off though. We've got, what, a week? That's barely enough time to have more drywall delivered, let alone install it."

Viv looked at the room thoughtfully, "I'm not sure what drywall has to do with Thanksgiving."

Emma chuckled. "You're right. We can light it with candles and the 'otherworldly glow of the undead.'"

"Now you're talking," Viv said, wedging one of the box fans into an open window. As she set up the dehumidifier, Emma walked into the kitchen where she found a stack of the captain's manuscript pages on the table. The paper undulated, like it had gotten wet and then dried out.

"No wonder he was so mad last night," she muttered to herself as she picked up the pages and began to read.

Sassy's eyes opened slowly. The gray light of the early morning hours filtered in through the window. He got out of bed, stretched, and padded over to the window.

He turned to look at Colin. His friend was asleep, his head pillowed on his paws. Sassy hesitated for a moment. He had never been the paternal type. But Colin was special.

He didn't know if the young cat knew what he was in for —didn't know if he'd be up for the job. But Sassy had been young once. He remembered. Someone took a chance on him once.

"Colin."

The young cat opened his eyes and yawned. "Yeah?"

"Time to get up. The Sandpiper wants to buy off the force? Let him. There are cats he can't buy off. We're getting the team back together."

"The team?"

"Billy Bear: artiste of the rough handshake. Fights best when the odds are against him."

"I remember my dad said something about him."

"Twinkletoes: infiltration and exfiltration expert. Can pick a lock with a whisker."

"Didn't he serve time for a charge down in—?"

"Miss Kitty," Sassy shook his head and let out a low whistle, "has eyes and ears in every back room and two-bit nip joint in this city."

"But aren't all those operatives… retired?"

"Legends. They're legends, kid. They're going to help you and me take down the Sandpiper."

Colin's eyes widened. "You're going to take him down?"

"I'm going to kill him."

Colin was silent for a moment. "I'm in."

Sassy looked at Colin. The young cat was eager and full of energy. But was he ready for this? "You sure about that?"

"Yeah. I'm sure."

"Okay then. Let's assemble the team."

They left the safety of the sewer and hit the streets. Sassy had a plan, and he was going to see it through. He was going to take down the Sandpiper once and for all.

CHAPTER 40
SLOW SPEED CHASE

"He's getting better at writing, I think," Viv said, making Emma jump.

"Don't sneak up on me like that!" She set the pages back down. "You're right though. He's getting better. I wonder if he'll try to get an agent."

"Can he do that? He's a cat."

Emma laughed. "We don't ask questions like that in this family. Hey, that reminds me of something Al said. He was surprised people could be in the same room with their siblings."

"It is a little surprising. I can barely stand to talk to my brother. We're like water and oil."

"The other day, Al mentioned that he has a sister."

"Really? It's a good thing she's not here. Riley's having a hard enough time keeping Al under control."

"Oh my god."

"What?"

Emma's heart raced. "I have an idea. Will you come with me?" She walked to the kitchen, grabbed a trash bag, and began stuffing the mess of shredded pink paper into it. "I think I've found the missing puzzle piece." Emma dropped the bag by the front door and ran up the stairs.

"Sure thing," Viv called after her, confused. "Where are we going?"

When Emma returned, she was holding a large book to her chest. "I need to take something back to the library."

———

Emma took the steps up to the library two at a time. Under her arm was the *Tattler* collection. Viv followed behind her with the bag of pink confetti.

Emma hoped this would work. If it didn't, she was going to look like a fool in front of Viv, and that possibility bothered her more than she expected.

She opened the library door and walked into the gleaming foyer. The marble floor gleamed in the afternoon light. It was spotless and freshly polished. *Just like I expected.*

Display cases held books for back to school, a paper wasp nest, a microscope, and a model of the solar system. The walls were lined with cork boards, which were covered in crisp construction paper collages featuring the word of the day (cummerbund), the plant of the day (ficus), and a motivational quote (A peacock that rests on its tail feathers is just another turkey.) None of it had been there last night.

When she pushed through the large double doors which led to the library's main room, she knew what to expect, but she still gasped.

It was, in a word, everything you hoped that a small-town library could be. In the front, polished study tables stood next to displays of staff recommendations. It hardly mattered that none of the books were less than forty years old.

Beyond the tidy reference desk and the card catalog were shelves of books neatly arranged.

"Whoa, somebody's really fixed up this place."

"I was here last night with Riley. It was nowhere near this perfect then. The books were on the floor. None of the displays were here."

"It has to be magic, doesn't it?"

"No, I don't think so. I think it's Al's sister. You said it yourself: you and your brother are like oil and water. Al's a chaos demon, so his sister must be an order demon."

"There are order demons?"

"It's time to find out." Emma turned addressed the room. "Hello? I'm returning your book. I didn't know it belonged to you. I'm going to put it on the table. You might as well come out. I only want to talk."

Nothing happened. After a moment, Viv spoke. "It was a good try—"

"No, I expected this. Al is flamboyant, which means his sister will be shy. That's why I brought a secret weapon." Emma took the trash bag from Viv, plunged her arm inside, grabbed a handful of confetti and threw on the floor. She walked all over the room, scattering the shredded paper randomly. When the bag was empty, she gestured for Viv to follow her into the foyer.

When the door to the foyer closed behind them, Emma ducked down and peered through its window into the main room.

A tidy, gray-haired woman emerged from the stacks and examined the mess, shaking her head. A pair of reading glasses hung from a beaded necklace around her neck.

"Why are people always so messy," she mumbled. Then she… changed.

The woman's hands seem to blur together. She was every-where at once. It was impossible to tell if she was simply fast, or if she had somehow spread out to encompass the room.

When the woman was finished, she assumed her normal form again and stood. She was holding a stack of pink pages. She squared them up and set them neatly on the table.

Emma turned to Viv. "Now."

"Now what?" Viv said, but Emma was already through the door, swooping up the pages from the table and pursing the strange woman, who had seen her and was fleeing toward the stacks.

Emma caught up with her easily and matched pace. "Excuse me."

"I can't hear you, dear," the woman shuffled imperceptibly faster. "Oh, why did I choose to manifest in this blasted form? You won't catch me! I won't allow it."

"Catch you? I only wanted to talk."

The woman veered suddenly to her left through a door that said EMPLOYEES ONLY. Emma followed.

"Can't you read the sign? Employees only! You humans have no respect for anything. You *say* you only want to talk, and then the next thing I know I'll be tied to a stake and wondering why my feet are so warm."

"We're Al's friends," Viv said, catching up to them.

The woman frowned. "Never heard of him."

"Your brother. Chaos demon? Kind of insufferable? Anyway, it doesn't matter. I just wanted to say thank you for reassembling these papers."

The woman stopped so suddenly that others nearly rearended her. She turned, slowly raising an eyebrow. "Where, exactly, is my brother?"

"Getting ready for a play."

"Oh, so he's an actor now, is he?" The woman scoffed. "Last century, it was hot-air balloons. Before that, fencing. I keep telling him that he'll never amount to anything if he can't stick to it for at *least* a millennium."

"So you've been a librarian before? You've done amazing things with this place."

"How could I not? It was in a disgraceful state. Nothing like the library of Alexandria," she said, wearing a far-off look. "Now, young lady, tell me why you made such a mess in my library?"

"It was the only way I knew to get your attention. And I was hoping you could reassemble the document for me." Emma rifled through the pages. "I'm amazed there isn't more missing."

"Well, I'm glad I could *impress* you," the woman said, rolling her eyes.

"This is the one thing that's gone right for me lately," Emma said. Then she glanced at Viv. "Well, not the only one. My house might be trashed, but at least I have friends to help me pick up the pieces."

"Trashed, you say?" the woman flashed a hungry look, which Emma didn't like.

"We'll let you get back to your library. Thanks again for your help." Emma was about to grab Viv and scram, but she changed her mind. "You know, I think Al—your brother—would like it if you were at the performance."

"He would?"

"He's mentioned you a couple of times. I think he looks up to you."

"I'll… consider it."

"The day and time are still undecided," Emma said, glancing down at the papers, "though I wouldn't be surprised if it happens sooner than you'd think."

They said goodbye and left. Emma glanced over her shoulder and saw the woman happily shelving the volume of the *Tattler* she'd returned.

Emma's heart raced as she flew down the stairs with Viv. Her right hand held the documents printed on pink paper. Thanks to the order demon, she had a list of every building in the core along with their owners' names. One of these names belonged to a killer—she only had to prove it.

CHAPTER 41
THE PLAY'S THE THING

Back at Deadtown Coffee, they found the troupe where they'd left them. Dash, unseen by the others, gave a little wave to Emma. The rest of them were arguing about how many candles would be needed to illuminate the stage and if *real* candles would be too much of a fire hazard. They didn't notice when Emma stormed up to them.

"The play's the thing!" she shouted.

"That's what I'm talking about!" Viv shouted too.

Everyone stopped talking and looked at Emma and Viv. Riley eventually broke the silence. "What are you talking about?"

"I mean, the play's the thing!"

"Yeah, I understand. You're quoting *Hamlet*. 'The play's the thing wherein I'll catch the conscience of the king.' What I'm asking is *why* are you quoting *Hamlet*?"

"Because I know who the murderer is. I found the missing puzzle piece, and now everything fits together."

"Great. Then you should give the info to the cops."

"I tried talking with them before, but they wouldn't listen because they think the case is solved. The only way to make them realize their mistake is to get the *real* killer to confess. I have an idea—"

"I'm not sure I like where this is going."

"You were going to restage the play. You said you could do it anytime. I'm suggesting that we do it tomorrow, in the old theater."

Riley leaned back in their chair and did some mental calculations. "It would be a stretch... but we could pull it off. Tell me again exactly *how* you expect to make the killer confess?"

"We're going to make a few changes to the script. I think Al might enjoy them."

"Delightful!" the demon gushed.

"We'll have to put it up to a vote of course," Riley said, looking at each cast member in turn. "All in favor?"

Every hand shot up.

"I guess we're doing it," Riley said. "But how are you going to make sure the murderer watches the play?"

Emma grinned. "Thanks, guys; you're the best. As for the killer, leave that to Viv and me. We've talked about it. We're going to make some flyers."

"Then I guess there's no time to waste," Riley said, turning to the cast. "If we're going to do this, let's do it! Astrid, we're going to need a few more hands. Call the undergraduates. Tell them it's twenty points extra credit on the final. Everybody else, let's meet at the theater in half an hour. Move!"

A moment later, the back room was empty of everyone except Emma and Viv.

"Hey, Em," Viv asked. "Do you really think this will work?"

Emma exhaled. "I sure hope it does."

CHAPTER 42
AFFORDABLE HOUSING

The late morning was unseasonably clear as Emma left her house, carrying a grocery bag. It contained a ridiculous garment that she'd hemmed by hand last night.

Walking across the green, she saw a familiar figure waiting by the fountain. He was wearing his usual tweed sport coat and a less habitual exasperated look.

"Hi, Marcus. Are you coming to the play?"

"You know as well as I do that Viv asked me to meet you here. Emma, what on earth are you mixed up in?"

"I've thought about what you said the other night… about the benefit of the doubt, about how I've been lucky. You're right; I have been lucky."

"Well, I'm not used to hearing that," Marcus said with a smile.

Emma gestured to the far side of the park where her colorful Victorian row house gleamed. "Just look at my house. I was only able to afford it because my aunt left me an inheritance. And I was only able to buy it so cheaply because I got in before people like Reinhold could drive up prices. That got me thinking. What if ordinary working people had a chance to buy the empty houses in the core while they're still affordable?"

"Believe me, I've thought of it. But these houses were abandoned forty years ago. Most of the original owners have moved away. Many of them have died. I know plenty of families who'd love to buy one of these houses, but they could never afford to track down who owns them."

She pulled a manila folder from her bag and handed it to him. "Here's something that should help with that."

"What's this?"

"Let's just say it's a little present from Reinhold Industries," she said when he extracted the pink pages from the envelope and skimmed through them.

"How did you get this?" he asked.

"I'm not sure you'd believe me," she grinned. "If I were you, I'd make a copy as soon as possible. The county sheriff's going to want the original."

"Don't tell me—"

"What? That the murderer's name is on that list?"

"I *said* don't tell me. Okay—but now you can tell me. Who are we talking about here?"

"You should really come to the play." She winked, tilting her head toward the crowd of curious Undertowners who were starting to gather outside the old theater. "Speaking of which, I've got legs to break."

CHAPTER 43
FACE-OFF

Emma waded through the crowd that had formed in front of the theater. It was surprisingly large for such a last-minute production. Diedre waved at her, apparently returned from her self-imposed exile. All the board members from the Neighborhood Association were there except for the secretary, Gladys—and their chairman, Clarence, of course. Even the captain looked on from the sidelines, standing with Rue, Bob, and Lily from the Ghost Hunters' Club.

The main emotion she sensed in the crowd was curiosity. Were they really going to restage the play after what happened the first time? How could they do it in a run-down theater without electricity? Who would be willing to play Caesar? Would there be *another* murder?

Emma pushed through the crowd to the theater's front entrance, noting appreciatively that the door was plastered with the flyers she and Viv made last night.

The flyers simply stated that the Undertown Players were restaging *Julius Caesar* to make up for the previous aborted production. It would take place at the old theater.

Well, that wasn't *all* they said.

At the bottom of the flyers were eleven small words Emma knew would draw the killer to the performance: *Made possible by a grant from Reinhold Industries' Undertown revitalization initiative.*

Emma jumped back as the door cracked open. "Where have you been?" Riley hissed. "You missed my pregame psych-up. I gave a great speech."

"That sounds—"

"No time for small talk. Come in and get into costume!"

Emma slipped through the door and followed Riley through the foyer, down the aisle, and to the backstage.

To say that the place had been transformed would be an understatement. It had been a dank, foreboding building. Now it was inviting.

The balconies and wings of the main level had been blocked off by huge swathes of gray fabric that hung from the ceiling and swayed gently. The seats directly in front of the stage were clean. The dust had been removed from their velvet, and their metal parts had been made to shine. But the most spectacular change was the lighting. The isles were lined with mason jars and filled with smooth, green-glass pebbles. At the bottom of each jar, a battery-powered tea light flickered. Together, they filled the space with a gentle, underwater kind of light.

Riley saw Emma staring. "Al was upset that we couldn't use *real* candles of course, but I think these worked out."

"I'm just amazed you were able to do all this overnight."

"We called in the undergrads. You'd be surprised what they would do for a few points of extra credit."

"Isn't that… unethical?"

"Not at all. They're getting invaluable experience in the field of practical folklore. I mean, we have a *real* demon."

"Actually, we have two."

Riley stopped midstride. "What? Never mind. You can tell me later, but for now, the show must go on. You need to get into costume and take your position. You'll have to do it back here since the dressing rooms are full of pigeon droppings. I'm going to go open the doors and let the people in."

As Emma shimmied into her toga, she felt butterflies in her stomach. She hadn't exactly *wanted* to be a part of the show, but nobody else was willing to play the role of Caesar after the last Caesar was killed—especially not with the changes she'd made to the script.

She joined the other actors and peeked out from behind the curtain. The crowd from outside had almost finished filing in and finding seats. There, sitting in the front row, was the person she'd hoped to see.

"Excuse me."

Emma turned to see Riley wearing an impatient expression. She realized she was blocking the path to the stage and moved aside.

The undergraduates had cleaned up the sulfur pentagram. The only indication that a demon had ever been summoned here was the discolored spot where the aqua regia had spilled.

As Riley walked onto the stage, the air was filled with a ghoulish, greenish glow. *That's Dash's handiwork,* Emma thought as the room grew silent.

"Thanks, everyone, for coming to our new production of *Julius Caesar,*" Riley announced. "Think of it as a way for us to make amends. Our previous performance ended early with the murder of one of our actors. In this performance, there won't be any murders. Instead, we will reveal to you... a killer."

The theater went completely dark. A startled wave of hushed conversation filled the theater, fading only as the stage filled with diffused light to reveal the actors.

Astrid spoke the first lines of the play. "Hence! Home, you idle creatures, get you home! Is this a holiday? What, know you not, being mechanical, you ought not walk upon a laboring day without the sign of your profession? —Speak, what trade art thou?"

The tradesman, played by Al, replied in a meek voice. "Why, sir, a carpenter."

Emma used this opportunity to scan the crowd. Their faces were filled with curiosity and confusion. None of them had fled. *Oh well, we'll get them in the second round.*

"Caesar, you're on," Riley said, elbowing Emma in the ribs. "Remember: you're the emperor. No slouching."

Emma squared her shoulders and strode out onto the stage. Parts of the stage, lit by Dash's otherworldly glow, turned royal purple. *Dash—what will I tell him?* Emma frowned, then remembered her role and turned to the darkened audience.

She did not know what to say. Her lines, which a minute ago seemed so easy, now seemed as distant and trackless as the Sahara.

"Calpurnia," a voice hissed. It was Riley, prompting her from the wings. Like magic, the word oriented her. She found her footing. She was an emperor.

"Calpurnia."

"Peace, ho! Caesar speaks."

"Calpurnia."

"Stand you directly in Antonius's way when he doth run his course…"

The play was a blur to Emma. It didn't feel like something she was doing, but rather something she was caught up in. She was almost surprised when she heard herself say, "He is a dreamer. Let us leave him. Pass." That was her cue to exit.

"Not bad for a first performance," Riley said, handing her a small bottle of water as she left the stage. "How do you feel?"

"I feel okay. I… don't think I remember anything that just happened out there."

"That's normal. Trust me though; you did good. I kept an eye on the audience while you were busy. Nobody's left."

"Good. Now we just have to spring the trap."

Riley glanced out to the stage, then addressed a group of actors standing around, chatting. "Hey, I need Trebonius in position." They turned to Emma. "I need to run. Remember your cue."

Emma nodded, swigging the water. After what seemed like both an eternity and an instant, she heard the line she was waiting for.

"Run, Lucius, and commend me to my lord. Say I am merry. Come to me again and bring me word what he doth say to thee."

Emma set the bottle of water on a folding table and swallowed. Her mouth was dry. She walked back on stage. *Remember, you're an emperor.* "The ides of March have come!"

She recited her lines automatically and went through the motions of the play as she waited for the turning point to arrive. Finally, it was time. She readied her line. "Doth not Brutus bootless kneel?"

Al had insisted on playing Brutus. He stood and walked toward Emma, drawing out of his toga an enormous dagger.

Emma's eyes widened. Al's dagger looked nothing like the cardboard daggers they'd used in rehearsal. It was made of something translucent and sharpened so finely that when its edge caught the light, it seemed like a bright gash had been cut in the world.

Al raised the dagger over Emma, then winked at her. Suddenly, his face began to change. His jaw became narrower. His protruding brow became flat. His skin became wrinkled and droopy. He had changed into the face of a killer: Gladys.

The audience gasped as the room went dark. Emma stood, heart pounding, ready to chase her quarry if she ran. But as the lights came up, she heard a single person clapping.

"Bravo!" Gladys called from the front row. "Really, quite a

spectacular performance. Of course you will be hearing from my lawyers when I sue you for defamation, but don't let me stop you. Please keep going."

Emma clenched her hands into fists as she looked down from the stage at Gladys. The woman was enjoying this.

"We made a deal, Gladys," a slippery kind of voice rolled out from the back of the wooden stage and filled the room. *Thump, thump, thump.* A man in dress shoes, slacks, and a perfectly starched white shirt, covered in blood, strolled forward.

It was Harold Loftus.

He jumped casually down from the stage and walked slowly toward Gladys, whose face was frozen in shock. "I thought it was a fair deal too. I take care of Reinhold. You take care of the Neighborhood Association. We buy up the core for pennies on the dollar, fill it up with luxury condos, and retire—each to our own private island."

He stopped in front of Gladys's seat, continuing. "But you got greedy. You wanted to be queen, so you came up with a plan to get us all out of the way."

"You're not Harold," Gladys spat, though her face betrayed her fear. "Harold is dead. You're just someone in a silly mask."

The man leaned forward until his face was an inch away from hers. "I see it was a mistake to make myself more presentable. You want to see what I *really* look like these days?"

From the stage, Emma couldn't see what Harold did, but she saw the color drain from Gladys's face. Then she slipped out of her chair and bolted toward the exit, frantically looking over her shoulder at Harold, who followed her as if he had all the time in the world.

She pushed on the exit door. It didn't open. She pushed again, throwing her whole body into it, but the door was unmoved. Meanwhile, Harold caught up with her.

"What do you want from me!" she wailed, no longer fully in control of her emotions. "Do you want me to apologize? I can't, because I'm *not* sorry. You're an awful man, Harold. Tricking Clarence into killing you was a mercy compared to what you deserved. If you want revenge, well, here I am! Take it... if you're man enough."

The house lights came on, and Emma walked up to Gladys, who was huddled against the door. "That won't be necessary. We don't want revenge. We want justice."

Gladys regarded Emma bitterly and opened her mouth to speak. But before the words had a chance to form, the door behind her opened and sent Gladys sprawling. Viv peeked in her head in. "Hey, guys, did we get her?"

CHAPTER 44
BIG SISTER

"Once again, I have outdone myself." Al said, clapping his hands together and resting them on his heart. "Was that not the finest example of acting you have ever seen?"

"As much as it pains me to say it," Riley answered, "you were amazing."

"You were," agreed another voice—one newly familiar to Emma. Everyone turned toward the newcomer: a tidy, older woman with gray hair and reading glasses dangling from a chain around her neck. "I... never imagined you could do something like this," the order demon made a gesture encompassing the whole room. "It's clear to me that even after millions of years, I still have a lot to learn about my brother."

Al was for once too stunned to speak, tears glistening in the corners of his eyes.

"We should be going soon," his sister said, "but first—"

"Why does Al have to go home?" Emma interrupted. "It seems pretty clear that he wants to be in the theater."

"Thank you, Emma," Al said. "But having tread upon these boards and having given the most inspired performance this verdant world of yours has ever seen, it's only right for me, now, to retire. It's time for me to return to my home. I'll teach them what I've learned here. Perhaps, one day, I'll invite all of you to the opening performance of the Nether Regions Theater!"

"Now, brother, that's an admirable goal. But I'm not quite ready to return home. There's a little organizing I need to finish."

Emma smiled at the two demons. Though one was aligned with order and the other with chaos, you could see the family resemblance. Emma left them and wandered over to Marcus, who was sitting with an utterly defeated-looking Gladys.

"We're waiting for the county to show up. They're not going to be happy about having so much egg on their face. I still don't quite understand though how you figured out it was Gladys."

"There're lots of reasons. With the chairman gone, she became interim chair of the Neighborhood Association and immediately tried to pass a resolution that would bring the Seattle Police into Undertown—"

"We *will* pass it!" the old woman said, more to herself than Emma.

"She also owns several valuable properties, both on Main and in the Core, which meant she knew about real estate and would be alerted when a stranger showed up in town and started asking questions about vacant buildings." Emma glanced at the manila envelope tucked under Marcus's arm. "And then there was the glitter."

"Glitter?" Marcus asked.

"It gets everywhere. No matter how much you clean, you can never get all of it out," Emma said dryly. "A few days ago, I was helping Gladys get home after a sprained ankle. A prankster had glitter bombed me, and some of it must have transferred to her. If you go back to the scene of the second murder, you'll find glitter on the windowsill where Gladys climbed onto the roof and waited to lure the man in the brown suit to his death."

"You think you know everything." Gladys looked at her and spat. "Your kind is always the same. You go to school. You get your fancy degrees, and you come back and lord it over everybody."

"No, I don't know everything," Emma said. When Gladys eyed her curiously, she explained. "I know *how* you killed the man in the brown suit, but I don't know why."

Gladys grinned like a crocodile. "Clarence had an overdue library book." The corners of her mouth lifted, and she broke into an unhinged cackle that continued long after Emma walked away.

CHAPTER 45
THE GIFT

Emma looked around at the crowd of friends sitting at the dining table in her new dining room. The table's richly polished wood shone in the flickering light from the imitation candles in the chandelier.

In front of each person was a place setting consisting of a lace doily, a bone china plate, two forks, two spoons, a butter knife, and a tiny implement for eating escargot. They were not eating escargot, but one had to admit it looked fancy.

It was the perfect Thanksgiving dinner... if you ignored the fact that Thanksgiving was tomorrow, that the ceiling was missing, the floor was water swollen, and the chairs wobbled.

"I still can't believe that order demon got this place so clean," Viv said. "It's a shame she couldn't fix the ceiling."

"I believe her words were 'I work miracles, not plaster.'" Emma laughed. "Hey, did you hear that the county is going to release Clarence, Clarice, and Darla?"

"Already did," said Marcus as he buttered a roll. "They should arrive home this afternoon, just in time for Thanksgiving."

"By the way, Em, it's such a good idea to have Friends-giving today," Viv said.

"Marcus, don't fill up on bread," Marcus's mother interrupted. "The main course is coming any minute—I just hope they seasoned the food."

"Need I remind you, Mom, I'm a full-grown man? If I want to eat a roll, I'm gonna eat a roll. By the way, Emma, we've already put that list to good use. Five families who were about to be pushed out of the neighborhood have been able to buy houses in the core. We've got a dozen more in the works."

"That's awesome. I can't wait to have some actual neighbors!"

"What? We don't count?" Dash called to her from where he was sitting with Rue, Bob, and Lily.

She smiled, deciding for the moment that it was okay to put off telling him about what she learned in the *Tattler*, at least until she knew more about *everything* that had happened.

"Well, you're going to have a *theater* as a neighbor," Riley said. "A donor who wishes to remain unnamed cut us a check for fifty grand to get the utilities connected and start making the place usable."

Ding-dong, the front bell sounded.

"That's weird; I'm not expecting anyone else." Emma put her napkin on the table and went to answer the door.

Someone had left a small gift box on her front steps. As she picked it up, Viv arrived behind her. "What's that?"

"I don't know. It doesn't have a shipping label on it. Who could have brought it?" Emma looked out at the park in front of her house, but it was empty.

She picked up the box. It was wrapped in a paper the texture of red velvet and it had a gold ribbon tied ornately in large loops around it. She pulled on one end of the ribbon, and it fell away. She lifted the lid... and was enveloped in a cloud of glitter.

"I am going to murder that demon," Emma said, gritting her teeth.

"Is that even *possible?* Hey, look, something else is inside," Viv said, looking over Emma's shoulder.

Emma reached into the box and pulled out an old, weather-beaten, clothbound book. The title of the book was *A Historical Geography of Undertown*. But it wasn't the title that made Emma gasp—it was the author. Dashiell P. Gruber. "This is a book by… Dash?"

Glued to the inside of the book's cover was a little envelope, which held an index card filled with names and dates. "This is a library book," she said, glancing at the library in the distance.

"Hey, close the door. It's freezing out there." Viv looked at Emma, then glanced at the book. "Aren't you going to read it?"

Emma smiled, looked down at the book, and wondered what it would tell her about Dash's life. She carefully put it back into the box and set the box on a side table. "The book's waited this long to find me; it can wait until tomorrow. Now it's Friendsgiving. Let's get back to our friends."

They walked back into the dining room just in time to see Emma's mom bring in a large, roasted turkey. Within just a few moments, she began to serve it to her smiling friends.

———

Years later, when each of them looked back on that day, they would forget that it hadn't *really* been Thanksgiving. They would forget about the missing ceiling and the uneven floor. They would even forget that the turkey really *had* been under seasoned and that the pumpkin pie had burned.

Instead, they would remember the laughter of their friends and the camaraderie after an ordeal. They would remember the relief of everything working out in the end.

And when they talked about that day, there would be a word that sprang automatically to their lips: *perfect.*

It was the perfect Thanksgiving dinner.

NEXT IN SERIES:

Sus Sasquatch

Buy Sus Sasquatch direct from the author at tabathagray.com

Welcome to the winter festival! Hot cider, tarot, and old friends await. But when a shocking find sends the neighbors fleeing, is it murder or something wilder?

On the other side of Undertown, robbery spills an ally's secret. Stolen magic promises answers to any fool who follows the trail. Good thing Emma's on the case!

She may be the worst psychic in the world, but she's sure to catch the killer and the thief. She's got pluck! Not to mention quirky friends: the gossip ghosts; a professor of applied folklore; a bad-news barista; and a hard-boiled detective cat.

She'll need all the help she can get because slumbering

eyes are waking. A stolen book whispers secrets that could ruin Emma's wonderful new life, even if she escapes...

Made in the USA
Middletown, DE
13 June 2024

55732085R00125